D0921325

HOMECOMING

TAKING (Book #4)
STALKING (Book #5)

RILEY PAIGE MYSTERY SERIES
ONCE GONE (Book #1)
ONCE TAKEN (Book #2)
ONCE CRAVED (Book #3)
ONCE LURED (Book #4)
ONCE HUNTED (Book #5)
ONCE PINED (Book #6)
ONCE FORSAKEN (Book #7)
ONCE COLD (Book #8)
ONCE STALKED (Book #9)
ONCE LOST (Book #10)
ONCE BURIED (Book #11)
ONCE BOUND (Book #12)
ONCE TRAPPED (Book #13)
ONCE DORMANT (Book #14)
ONCE SHUNNED (Book #15)
ONCE MISSED (Book #16)

MACKENZIE WHITE MYSTERY SERIES
BEFORE HE KILLS (Book #1)
BEFORE HE SEES (Book #2)
BEFORE HE COVETS (Book #3)
BEFORE HE TAKES (Book #4)
BEFORE HE NEEDS (Book #5)
BEFORE HE FEELS (Book #6)
BEFORE HE SINS (Book #7)
BEFORE HE HUNTS (Book #8)
BEFORE HE PREYS (Book #9)
BEFORE HE LONGS (Book #10)
BEFORE HE LAPSES (Book #11)
BEFORE HE ENVIES (Book #12)
BEFORE HE STALKS (Book #13)

HOMECOMING

A Chloe Fine Psychological Suspense Mystery—Book 5

BLAKE PIERCE

Copyright © 2019 by Blake Pierce. All rights reserved. Except as permitted under the U.S. Copyright Act of 1976, no part of this publication may be reproduced, distributed or transmitted in any form or by any means, or stored in a database or retrieval system, without the prior permission of the author. This ebook is licensed for your personal enjoyment only. This ebook may not be re-sold or given away to other people. If you would like to share this book with another person, please purchase an additional copy for each recipient. If you're reading this book and did not purchase it, or it was not purchased for your use only, then please return it and purchase your own copy. Thank you for respecting the hard work of this author. This is a work of fiction. Names, characters, businesses, organizations, places, events, and incidents either are the product of the author's imagination or are used fictionally. Any resemblance to actual persons, living or dead, is entirely coincidental. Jacket image Copyright eldar nurkovic, used under license from Shutterstock.com.

BLAKE PIERCE

Blake Pierce is author of the bestselling RILEY PAGE mystery series, which includes fifteen books (and counting). Blake Pierce is also the author of the MACKENZIE WHITE mystery series, comprising thirteen books (and counting); of the AVERY BLACK mystery series, comprising six books; of the KERI LOCKE mystery series, comprising five books; of the MAKING OF RILEY PAIGE mystery series, comprising five books (and counting); of the KATE WISE mystery series, comprising six books (and counting); of the CHLOE FINE psychological suspense mystery, comprising six books (and counting); and of the JESSE HUNT psychological suspense thriller series, comprising five books (and counting).

ONCE GONE (a Riley Paige Mystery—Book #1), BEFORE HE KILLS (A Mackenzie White Mystery—Book 1), CAUSE TO KILL (An Avery Black Mystery—Book 1), A TRACE OF DEATH (A Keri Locke Mystery—Book 1), and WATCHING (The Making of Riley Paige—Book 1) are each available as a free download on Amazon!

An avid reader and lifelong fan of the mystery and thriller genres, Blake loves to hear from you, so please feel free to visit www.blakepierceauthor.com to learn more and stay in touch.

TABLE OF CONTENTS

PROLOGUE

Sherry Luntz wasn't much for sentiment, but she was one for celebration. It was why she was slightly breaking the speed limit on her way home from work. She had two steaks in one bag in the passenger seat and a bottle of red wine in another. Tonight was her anniversary; she'd been married to Bo Luntz for twenty-one years now and this was the first anniversary they'd be sharing without their son in the house. She'd hoped not having Luke live with them any longer would have spiced things up in their marriage, but it had not. If anything, it seemed to have drawn a wedge between her and Bo.

It had been two weeks since they'd last slept together, and that had been a very quick non-event in the morning before work. But dammit... it was her anniversary and she was going to get some tonight. If he didn't come for her, she had ordered an especially slutty little thing online last week that she was going to use to essentially attack him.

She arrived home at 5:25, about five minutes earlier than she usually arrived home from work. Bo's truck was in the driveway, which meant he was already home, too. This was nothing new, as he usually arrived home before she did.

As she parked the car and got out, it occurred to her that Bo might not even realize today was their anniversary. He was pretty good with remembering special dates, but he'd seemed off lately. Ever since Luke had left for college, Bo seemed distant and simply not himself.

Still... if he somehow forgot that this was their anniversary, she was going to be pissed. But because she also wanted to jump his bones quite badly, she figured she could wait until tomorrow to be mad.

She went inside and found the house quiet. Entering the con-joined living room and kitchen area, she saw that Bo was not there. This was odd because almost every afternoon, he was either at the kitchen table answering last-minute emails from work, or sitting on the couch catching up on the day's news.

She was confused at first but then a smile touched her lips. Perhaps he not only knew it was their anniversary but was just as excited as she was about it. She set the steaks and wine on the kitchen counter and slowly made her way up the staircase that was situated between the living room and kitchen. She knew Bo was not the type of man to use rose petals or soft music to seduce her. Neither of them were particularly romantic.

And Sherry was fine with that. Honestly, she'd be just as happy if he jumped out at her from behind the bedroom door and took her right then and there against the wall. The mere thought of this got her excited, causing her to speed up as she neared the top of the stairs.

"Bo?" she asked, putting a bit of playfulness into her voice.

She passed the bathroom and came to their bedroom door. It was closed and she tried to remember if she had closed it upon leaving that morning. Too excited to even think about it clearly, she opened the door, fully expecting to have him grab her or, if she was really lucky, for him to be spread out on the bed naked and waiting.

She got neither of those things. She frowned and turned back to the hallway. *Where the hell is he?*

It then dawned on her that she had texted him to let him know she was bringing steaks home. She'd almost ended the text with *"for our anniversary"* but had decided against it, hoping he remembered on his own. Given that he knew she was bringing steaks, he was probably out on the patio, firing up the grill.

A little let down by not getting a surprise in the bedroom, Sherry walked back downstairs. She nearly went ahead and started getting together the spices and seasoning for the steaks but decided she'd rather see Bo first. Maybe she'd give him a juicy kiss to plant the seeds for what she expected later in the night.

She opened the patio door and stepped outside. She was closing the door behind her when she saw Bo. And at first, it made no sense.

He was lying on the patio, facing the door. His eyes were wide and unblinking and there was something dark sticking out of his mouth—something soft and round. She tried to make sense of what was in his mouth but that's when she realized that there was a pool of blood around his head. It was a very dark shade of red and it was still wet.

"Bo ...?"

Of course, Bo did not respond.

Sherry felt a scream crawling up out of her throat. When it finally came out, she realized that she could smell lighter fluid and warming charcoal. Bo *had* come out to start the grill. Suddenly, the smell of the charcoal was the only thing she was aware of as she fell to her knees, screaming in agonized wails next to her dead husband.

CHAPTER ONE

"This is Danielle... do your thing at the beep."
Chloe ended the call and set her cell phone down on the bar top. She looked out the window of the bar she had randomly selected. She was drinking alone on a Thursday afternoon, just two days after closing her last case. She was still sore from the outcome, but that was the last thing on her mind. Staring out the window at the late afternoon hours washing golden sunlight over the streets of DC, Chloe was beginning to worry about Danielle.

She hadn't spoken to her sister in two days. She knew that two days was really nothing to get concerned about but the way things had gone between them lately, she could not help but worry. Besides, it wasn't just that Danielle had apparently turned her phone off; Chloe had gone by her apartment as well and no one had answered.

Chloe drained her second beer of the afternoon and looked at the clock on her phone. It was 5:17—a full half hour after the last time she'd checked. She couldn't remember the last time she'd felt such worry, such a need to constantly keep up with the time.

She was vaguely aware of the bartender approaching her. He nodded to her empty glass and said: "Another?"

She almost said yes. Chloe did not get drunk often but she wondered if she'd stop worrying if she just kept drinking and drinking. Maybe she'd get so drunk she'd take a cab home, pass out, and then wake up tomorrow to realize that she had been worried for nothing.

But this is not like her. This is not like the new Danielle I have been getting to know.

"No thanks," she said. "Just my tab."

He went to the register to retrieve it as Chloe picked her phone back up. Her call history was proof of just how much she'd been worrying—especially this afternoon. She'd even gone so far as to call the strip club where Danielle worked as a bartender. And it was then when she had truly started to worry. Danielle's manager had informed her that Danielle had called in sick two days ago, reporting mono or some sort of sore throat.

But if that was the case, she was not holing up at home. And she was not answering her phone. It didn't make much sense to turn off your phone when you were suffering from an illness, now did it?

The bartender handed her the bill and she slid her credit card over. As she signed the receipt, she wondered if she should file a missing person's report. It would be dumb; if someone filed one for a similar situation and she had the run of it, she'd likely roll her eyes and ignore it. Besides ... because of Danielle's history, a missing person's claim was the last thing she needed. Based on Danielle's history, it wouldn't be much of a stretch to assume she had decided to just pack up and move somewhere else.

No, not this new Danielle ...

Chloe left the bar more frustrated than before. She tried to decide on one particular emotion—worry or frustration—but found they actually worked irritatingly well together. As she started walking toward her apartment, she tried to convince herself that she was being stupid. She hated that she was so convinced that something was wrong. She had never been the worrying type, always looking for some logical reason *not* to worry in any given circumstance. She was sure that as soon as she stopped obsessing over this, Danielle would call and tell her that she'd just skipped town to see some of her old friends up in Maryland or something.

Just as this flimsy reassurance crossed her mind, her phone rang.

He heart leaped at once. She was so absolutely certain it was Danielle that she didn't even bother checking the caller display. She even had to catch herself from speaking her sister's name as she answered it.

"Hello?"

"Agent Fine … hey," said a male voice. It took her a moment to place it and when she did she felt bad for being so disappointed. It was Kyle Moulton. Any other time, she might have been pleased to hear from him, but having been so eager to hear from her sister, it was almost a non-event to hear from him.

"Hi, Moulton."

"Sorry to call out of nowhere but I had some downtime. They usually let me make calls around this time, about twice a week, and I thought I'd check in to see how you were doing."

"I'm good." She paused here, cringing at her own lie and how utterly fictitious her words sounded. "You know what?" she said. "I'm actually struggling right now."

"Work?"

"No. Personal stuff."

"Ah, I see. Jeez, Fine. Last time we talked, that personal crap was eating at you, too. Things not getting any better?"

"For someone locked up and unable to support me emotionally, these are some pretty pressing questions you're asking."

He chuckled, though there wasn't much humor in it. "I know. Sorry. But hey, there are wheelings and dealings going on behind the scenes … all legal. Looks like my sentence might be shortened significantly. Though any chance of me coming back to work with the bureau seems very small."

"Well, here's hoping."

He was quiet for a minute and when he did start speaking again, he seemed very somber. "Hey, look … I just wanted to say hi. I didn't realize all of this personal stuff was still eating at you. I can call back some other time."

"No, you're fine. It's just … it's been a rough day."

She nearly told him about her suspicions concerning Danielle, thinking he might be able to offer some valuable advice. But she decided that it was a bit too personal—and that it showed a slightly paranoid side of her that she was not ready for Moulton to see.

"So…can I take it there's been no resolution with your dad, your sister, and the diary?"

"No…it's sort of…"

She stopped here—not just talking, but walking as well. Her apartment was just one block away now, but she had forgotten all about it.

"Fine?"

"Yeah…"

I didn't even think about Dad. I haven't spoken to him in a while…certainly not over the last few days…

"Moulton…you've helped me maybe stumble onto something here. I need to go."

"Hey, I'm just glad to have helped," he said with a bit of cheer. "Bye, Fine."

Chloe ended the call and then pulled up her father's number right away. She placed the phone to her ear and heard only a beat of silence, followed by his voicemail greeting. She stood there for a moment, trying to make a decision—trying not to overthink things and assume the worst.

But honestly, none of this was adding up. Given how badly her father seemed to want to make amends, there was no reason at all for him to avoid her calls. Sure, it was a stretch to assume that he, too, had skipped town or gone missing, but the fact that she was getting the same response from Danielle…it was too much to ignore.

Chloe pocketed her phone and sprinted the rest of the way to her apartment. Her worry was now morphing into fear and she suddenly sensed that every passing minute could potentially make the mystery even worse.

CHAPTER TWO

Exactly sixteen minutes passed between Chloe receiving the call from Moulton and the moment she parked in front of her father's apartment. His car was there, which was a good sign, she supposed. But it did very little to ease the flutter of panic that seemed to be growing minute by minute. She ran up the stairs and knocked on the door with urgency.

She waited several seconds and got no answer. She tried again, rapping loudly this time. She leaned in, her nose almost to the door, and said: "Dad, open the door."

Again, there was no answer. Expecting nothing, she tried the door and was surprised to find it unlocked. But as the door swung open, she realized how odd that seemed. And suddenly, the fact that the door was unlocked added yet another notch to her worry.

She stepped inside, closing the door behind her. The townhouse was quiet and tidy. She stepped into the living room, eyeing the place as if she did not quite trust it. She looked around for any signs that anything out of the ordinary had happened but could find nothing—other than the fact the front door had been unlocked.

She exited the living room and walked down the small hallway to his bedroom. Again, she could find nothing out of sorts. The bed was made and there was a small pile of dirty clothes by the side of the dresser. She realized that she was getting something of a private peek into her father's new life and it made her feel uncomfortable. She did not want to think of him as *new*; she'd come to terms with the kind of man he had truly been and as far as she was concerned, that was how she wanted to remember him always.

She left the bedroom, regretting her decision to come over here. But while she was here, she figured she might as well give the place a full once-over. She made her way into the kitchen and before she entered, she saw the first thing that looked out of place.

The teakettle was on the floor. There was no water around it and it was easily eight feet from where it should have been placed on the stove. Slowly, she bent over to pick it up. Her fingers hesitated in the air, hovering just a few inches away from the handle.

There was a smudge on the side—something that looked like a dark shade of red against the stainless steel body. It was not really a splatter, but more like a single drop of something, about the size of a quarter. It was a shade of dark red she had seen numerous times during her time with the bureau so she didn't even waste time wondering what it might be.

It was blood. It was *dried* blood, meaning it had been on the kettle for at least eight to ten hours. Probably longer.

She knelt by the teakettle and tried to come up with a hypothesis in her mind. The place she instantly wanted to go was that Danielle had come over for some reason and their father had attacked her—had perhaps driven off with her. But that made no sense because his car was still here. Also, if it was a planned attack and abduction, he would have been more careful about not leaving evidence behind. And the teakettle was a pretty glaring piece of evidence.

So if that's not what happened, what did happen?

She wasn't sure. There were many avenues to consider. One thing she did know was that with the unlocked door, the blood on the teakettle, and now *two* missing persons, she had enough speculative evidence to officially file a report.

Chloe took her phone from her pocket and nearly placed a call to Director Johnson. But that, she knew, would be a mistake. Any case that started this way was always handled by the local PD first. Even if she felt the bureau could better handle it because she knew the history behind the two missing people, it was a police matter—for now.

She called the police and as she listened to a woman answer the phone on the other end, she stared at that drop of blood and wondered if it belonged to her father or her sister.

It felt surreal to be the one being questioned. The detective who was taking her statement seemed to be very aware of what sort of ground he was treading on. Taking the statement of an FBI agent about a family-related issue could, after all, be a huge chance to put a gold star on his career. On the other hand, he was surely also aware that this FBI agent was likely sizing him up as he did his job.

Chloe felt bad for the guy, really… because she was sizing him up. He was very tall and somewhere near fifty years of age. He looked bored but also very alert—the same look she had seen in countless other detectives in the past.

He was doing a decent job, though he seemed dubious of the whole situation. He had arrived with two officers, both of whom were still looking the place over. Chloe was polite, not telling them that she had already done a thorough job of it.

"And you say the door was unlocked?" the detective asked her.

They were sitting on barstools in the kitchen, both looking the place over as if they might have missed something. "Yes," Chloe answered.

"Do you know if he usually left it unlocked?"

"No, I have no idea. It wouldn't seem likely, though. He's only been in DC for like a month. I doubt he felt safe and secure just yet."

"Can you think of any reason your father might have invited your sister over?"

She was not going to mention Danielle breaking into her own apartment to steal their mother's diary. Doing so would put Danielle under far too much scrutiny and it was her father who was the villain here. She was well aware it would impede the investigation, but she had no choice but to lie.

"None that I can think of," Chloe said. "Dad has been trying to reach back out to us, wanting to patch things up. We have a strained relationship, the three of us. Danielle was always a little more willing to buy his crap." There was the lie. "So maybe he just had her over to reconnect. I don't know."

"But judging from the teakettle and the blood on it, it might not have gone so well," the detective said.

"That's my worry."

"The only thing that bothers me is that the kettle is all we have," the detective said. "Yeah, there's blood there, but where's the evidence of a struggle?"

"I'd say the blood is the evidence."

"And you know for certain your father is the one who wielded it? Any chance that might be *his* blood?"

"Highly doubtful," Chloe said.

But even as he asked, she started to explore the other alternative—an alternative she had been blind to because she was so concerned with Danielle. If the door was unlocked and there was no sign of a struggle...more signs pointed to Danielle being the attacker rather than the attacked. She would have left in a hurry, neglecting to lock the door. And it would have been easier for her to get the drop on their father with the kettle because there was no way their dad would have even suspected she might attack him.

She kept this all to herself, though. She could not place Danielle in the position of being the attacker here. She noticed the detective eyeing her suspiciously, was if he knew where her mind was going. After a few moments he scribbled something in a little notepad he'd been holding the entire time, and got to his feet.

"Well, you know how this goes, Agent Fine," he said. "All we have to go on is that blood. We'll have it analyzed, as you know. And you can probably get the results faster than I can. But we'll collect it and get it going."

"Thanks."

"Also, please let us know if you think of anything else. If, you know...if anything else comes to mind."

His tone indicated that he felt like she was keeping something from him. But his expression also told her that he was fine with it. She was sure that being a detective in DC, he had at least encountered other agent-based cases or had worked with others who had. As far as Chloe knew, it could be common for him.

She had to remind herself of that. He was likely not seeing her as the panicked sister, but as a rational agent who knew there was a process. And damn it, she *did* know there was a process. She could not expect everyone to forget all the rules and regulations for something that was incredibly personal to her.

"I will," she said. "And thanks."

"In the meantime, we'll put an APB out on your sister and her car."

The detective walked off toward the bedroom to join the other officers. Chloe also got to her feet, unsure of where to go or what to do. She still felt certain her father was the one in the wrong here; Danielle had done some deplorable things in her past but Chloe did not think she was capable of murder.

Their father, however, was. Their past had proven this.

And if he and Danielle were together under tense circumstances, Chloe felt sure that there were no limits to what her father might do to ensure he remained a free man.

She headed for the door, figuring a trip to Danielle's place was the next logical step. Maybe she'd find some clues there, maybe some evidence that—

Her train of thought was once again interrupted by her cell phone. She grabbed it quickly, reading the name on the screen before answering this time. She was unsurprised to not see Danielle's name there, and was equally disappointed at the name she did see there.

Dir. Johnson.

She answered it with caution, not wanting Johnson to have any indication that she had called the police. The less Johnson knew about her family problems, the better.

"This is Fine," she answered.

"Fine, it's Johnson. You in town right now?"

"Yes, sir."

"Feeling well-rested? Did the past two days treat you well?"

"I'm feeling great, sir."

"Good. Look, I know it's short notice and pretty much stacked directly on top of your last case, but I need you to come in. I want to go over another potential case with you. It's pretty urgent, so I'd appreciate some speed."

She felt overwhelmed for a moment as she tried to imagine working another case with this whole new ordeal with Danielle and her father. But she knew if she declined to come in, Johnson would ask questions. And the more questions he asked, the closer to the truth he would come.

"I can be there in ten minutes," she said.

"Perfect."

Johnson ended the call, leaving Chloe to look around her father's apartment. She stood there in silence for a moment longer before finally heading for the door, feeling as if she was abandoning not only the mystery within, but her sister as well.

CHAPTER THREE

Danielle knew that she'd once led a toxic life—a life directed by her poor taste in men, her soft spots for excessive alcohol and drugs, and a distaste for authority. She knew this and she claimed it. Claiming it was, she knew, an important part of moving on from it. But one of the good things about that nasty past of hers was that it had kept her moving, from one residence to another. From one state to another.

Between the ages of seventeen and twenty-five, she had lived in nine different cities in five different states. That's how she knew about Millseed, Texas.

Millseed was a shithole. When she had lived here four years ago, the tiny town had been on its last legs. The population of under four hundred was barely enough to support the convenience store and general store that sat in the town's center like two splatted flies on a dusty windshield.

There wasn't even any real residential part of the town. There were several houses sporadically placed along the unmarked two-lane roads and then, just before the town limits promised better places beyond, there were two trailer parks. Danielle had lived in one of those parks for a very rough seven months of her life. Meth had been run through the park and how she had managed to avoid the lure of that particular drug was beyond her. The man she had been living with at the time had gotten addicted to it and was currently doing time in prison for multiple charges of distributing it.

But upon arriving in Millseed a little less than two days ago, Danielle had driven right by that trailer park. She was actually rather surprised the place was still standing. She'd ventured about a half a mile farther up the road, to a building that she had been told was once a slaughterhouse. It was a nondescript building tucked away behind a vacant lot overgrown with weeds, vines, and prickle bushes. The building looked even worse than she remembered it; its very bland and grimy appearance made it evident that it had once been used for nefarious purposes; after the slaughter of thousands of pigs, it had also been used for the creation of meth and second-rate ecstasy. She knew this because of the crowd she had once run with, the lame-ass crowd that had drawn her to Millseed in the first place.

But now Danielle wondered if she had been brought to Millseed for some other reason—perhaps some divine reason. She hated that it was the first place she thought of when she got her initial idea, but it *did* seem perfect.

Standing outside of the slaughterhouse and looking out across the overgrown field, she thought of how life sometimes seemed like a circle that brought her back to some place she had just narrowly escaped. She was smoking a cigarette, something she had not done since she had left this miserable excuse for a town, and thinking of what to do next.

She'd brought her father here to kill him and now she had reached the point of no return. A very large part of her wanted to call Chloe and fill her in. At the very least, she wanted her sister to know she was safe. She supposed she owed Choe *that* much.

Besides…what she had just done affected both of them. For Danielle, she assumed she'd never escape what she had done…that she would face the repercussions for the rest of her life. But for Chloe, it would be different. There would be a whole different kind of trauma there as she lived the rest of her life trying to understand why her sister had done such a thing.

Danielle hated that she missed Chloe. She'd lived nearly ten years of her life without her sister and had done just fine. Only, *just fine* was a hell of a stretch. She had *survived* during those years and nothing more.

She took one final drag from her cigarette, dropped it to the ground, and stomped it out. She hated the taste of it but the familiarity seemed fitting somehow. She'd gone through half a pack in the last day or so and while it helped calm her, it further convinced her that when she was done with the task at hand, she'd never be able to fully return to the habit.

When she walked back inside the slaughterhouse, it was like stepping into another world. Maybe one of those post-apocalyptic worlds that were so popular on TV these days. At some point in its past, the office end of the abattoir had been demolished and hauled off in pieces; small sections of concrete and scrap iron could be seen on the far edge of the field, nearly consumed by the thick and unyielding vegetation. The only thing that had been left behind was the large concrete rectangle where the slaughters had occurred. There were stains on the floor, all pointing in the direction of rusted metal grates in the floor. Even in her current mood, Danielle could not fathom the sorts of things that had gone sifting through those grates.

She walked across what she thought of as the "kill-floor" and to one of the two large chambers at the back of the building. They were separated from the kill-floor by only a half wall, creating separate rooms with easy access to the floor.

Inside this room, Aiden Fine hung by his arms from a rope that was connected to a metal track in the ceiling. Danielle assumed the tracks and ropes had, at one time, been used to tie pigs and slowly move them toward their death. For now, though, they were holding her father in place. His arms were held almost perfectly vertical, the rope bound around his wrists.

"Danielle," he said. "Please ... think about this You don't have to do this." His voice was haggard and dry. At least he wasn't crying anymore. God, she'd hated it when he had cried just as they had crossed over into Texas, the sounds of his weeping from the trunk even creeping in beyond her loud music.

"This again?" she asked. She sat on a low stack of old wooden pallets that had been tossed into the far corner. She looked at her father, understood that she had done this to him, and wondered what sort of monster she was becoming.

"Danielle, I..."

"You what?"

"I'm sorry."

She stepped toward him and looked him in his eyes. He was in pain from the way his arms were pulled upward and he was clearly tired. His feet were firmly on the ground but the angle his arms were forced to take surely made him more than a bit sore.

"Sorry for what?" Danielle asked.

He seemed to think about it for a moment. She wondered if he was actually considering whether or not he might admit to all of his crimes. But in the end, he said nothing. Danielle nodded with a frown and walked to the side of the room where she had a small plastic grocery bag. There were bottled waters and crackers inside. She opened one of the plastic bottles of water and walked over toward him.

"Open," she said.

He narrowed his eyes at her and for a brief moment, she thought she saw anger there. But it quickly turned to some sort of muted mercy as he opened his mouth for the first water he'd had in over twenty-four hours.

She slowly poured the liquid into his mouth and he swallowed it down greedily. She continued to pour until he started coughing against it. When she was done, Danielle recapped the water and returned to her stack of pallets.

"What do you want?" Aiden asked. "I don't know what you *think* I've done, but..."

"Let's not play dumb, Dad. You've had this coming for a while. I know it breaks your heart that I'm not the eight-year-old little girl you can bully and push around. It must sting to know you can't tower over me anymore. God...what I would have given to be able to do this to you back then..."

"This is about your mother?" He sounded almost surprised and that pissed Danielle off even more.

"Partly. Mostly. We know, Dad. We've seen the diary."

"What diary?"

Danielle slowly got off of her seat of pallets, walked over to him, and slapped him hard across the face. His body swayed a bit from the force of it, the rope and the overhead beam creaking.

"Try again," she said.

Aiden Fine looked around the empty room, startled and clearly trying to come up with some bullshit to keep her happy.

"Don't bother," she said. "I want the truth. We have the diary and we have read it. We know, Dad. We know everything."

She watched as his eyes tried to focus in on hers. She watched him cycle through a wellspring of emotions—from anger to fear to resentment. In the end, he chose helplessness.

"Please, Danielle. Think this through."

"I have," she said, turning her back on him. "Maybe a little too much."

She went back to the plastic bag and took two other items out: an unused shop rag and her mother's diary. She placed the diary on the stack of pallets and took the shop rag over to her father. Slowly, she pressed it against his mouth and pushed tightly. When all of the slack was out of it, she tied it around the back of his head, creating a crude but effective gag.

She then went back to the pallets, sitting down and opening up the diary. "Which parts would you like to hear first?" she asked. "The parts where Mom was pretty sure you were screwing another woman in her bed—that would be Ruthanne Carwile, in case you forgot— or how she was legitimately scared you were going to kill her?"

She took a great deal of pleasure in the moaning noises her father made through the gag. It made her think that her plan would pan out after all. She had ditched her phone, tossing it out the window somewhere in rural Virginia. Her car was parked behind the old slaughterhouse, tucked away in the overgrowth of what she assumed had once been a turnaround spot for delivery trucks.

She was basically invisible at this point. She had a tape recorder to catch his confessions and a gun to put a bullet between his eyes.

She had no delusions that he would simply give her a confession, and that was fine. She didn't mind making him sweat. The only question was how long she'd be able to remain patient.

She started reading. She did it whimsically, as if reading a toddler a bedtime story. She watched him to see if hearing the words made him squirm. Yes, she wanted him to hurt; she was okay admitting that. But it also made her wonder if she had ventured too far off the reservation—if she had finally stepped so far away from logic that there was no way to return.

CHAPTER FOUR

When Chloe arrived at Johnson's office, she entered to find Rhodes already there. She seemed to just have sat down, still adjusting herself in Johnson's notoriously uncomfortable guest chairs on the visitor's side of his desk. She gave Chloe a rather excited look that helped Chloe fall into place as well. She had to remind herself that if she was not knee deep in her own personal drama, she would have been thrilled to have been called in on what seemed to be a high-priority case.

Chloe took the other chair next to Rhodes. Johnson gave her a nod of appreciation on the other side of the desk while he typed in a few last words on his MacBook. With a sigh and an exaggerated slumping of his shoulders, he sat back in his chair and regarded them.

"Thank both of you for coming in so quickly, and on such short notice. We've got a case that I think the two of you could do very well on. We've got two murdered men within the span of four days, both in the suburbs of Baltimore. They were both middle-aged men, both married. So far, the cops are at a loss. It came across my desk and I instantly thought of the two of you."

Chloe looked at Rhodes. There was a look on her face that reminded Chloe of a rodeo bull, pushed against the gate and just waiting for it to be opened so it could go rampaging. It made what she was about to say even harder.

"Sir, I'm afraid I can't take a case right now." It hurt to say it; the words felt like barbed wire coming out of her throat.

Johnson smirked, and it was not a smirk of amusement. "Excuse me?"

"I was trying not to let this get in the way, but my sister is missing, sir. It's been almost forty-eight hours now. My father's missing, too."

Johnson blinked several times, as if trying to clear his head. She could see him struggling to figure out how her personal issues tied to this case. Director Johnson was a noble man and had always treated her well, but he was also the kind of man who firmly believed that the job came first, above anything else.

After a moment, he nodded. "I know. I got a call from a friend of mine, a certain detective that I believe you have just spoken to. He called to let me know what was going on—not because you were involved, but because it's a common courtesy he sometimes bestows upon me whenever he's investigating any sort of case that might have ties to the bureau. So yes...I know all about your sister, your father, and the little bit of evidence at the scene."

Chloe was absolutely gutted at hearing this. *So much for keeping my personal demons in their cages,* she thought.

"So then you understand," Chloe said.

Johnson shifted in his seat, rather uncomfortable. "What I understand is that you have a personal interest in the case, so you are overreaching. Based on what Detective Graves tells me, there was certainly some sort of altercation at the townhouse, but the case for kidnapping—which he thinks you are aiming for—is tenuous at best."

"Sir, surely you'd think differently if you knew the history and—"

"But I don't. And that's why I am trusting Graves and the police. If it turns out they think something else is at play there, they'll let me know. We can't treat it any different than any other police case, Fine."

Chloe felt rage welling up in her, but at the same time, some wiser part of her stepped up and took over. She understood what Johnson was doing and in an odd way, she almost appreciated it. He was trying to busy her; he was trying to distract her with work while the police looked for more answers pertaining to the disappearance of her sister and father. The fact that it did indeed seem to be the sort of case that she and Rhodes would be best served to take on made it only that much better.

"Fine...you have to let the cops do their job," Johnson said. "And while they do theirs, you need to focus on yours. Besides, even if I could muster the aloofness to let you go looking for your sister, there's no way I could let you meddle in a case that isn't even in the FBI's jurisdiction."

"But I could help."

"I'm sure you could. And if for some reason it ends up in the hands of the bureau, maybe I'll even let you oversee it."

"But sir..."

"I hate to be a jerk on this, Fine, but remember your place. You have a job and I expect you to do it. If you would like to take personal time, go ahead. I'll happily grant it. But if you do that and I find out you've been digging into your sister's case..."

He stopped here, letting her fill in the blanks. She knew he was right, but she was still irritated by just how cavalier he seemed to be over the fact that the sister of one of his agents was missing.

"So two choices for you, Fine. You either take some personal time off and wait around for the police to find some answers, or you go out to Baltimore with Rhodes and see if you can find us a killer."

And just like that, Chloe felt herself pushed into a corner. She knew if she took the personal time, she'd end up looking into her sister's disappearance. And until it was made a bureau issue—*if* it was made one at all—she could get into quite a bit of trouble for interfering in a case that was not the FBI's to solve.

Or she could busy herself with work. It was an easy choice to make, though her heart seemed to go rigid in defiance. "I want the case," she said.

"Good," Johnson said. "I feel for you, I really do. But I'd get in just as much of a bind as you if you were to get involved in this case."

"I know that, sir."

He nodded and waited a beat, as if to make sure she had nothing else to say on the matter. Chloe glanced over at Rhodes, noticing that her partner had gotten quite uncomfortable during the exchange. She looked like a kid who was sitting on the couch, waiting to see if the minor argument between mom and dad was going to escalate into a blow-out.

"As I was saying," Johnson said. "Two men dead within four days, both married. No leads, no clues … other than that they lived in the same area—within one and a half miles of one another, I believe."

He went through the details of the case—as usual, there weren't many—and Chloe did her very best to focus. But her thoughts never strayed far from Danielle and what she might be going through. She supposed she'd never be able to remove herself from it, no matter what kind of case she was assigned.

Not for the first time in her young career, she found herself deeply worried that her toxic family life was going to jeopardize her future in ways she could not control.

CHAPTER FIVE

After a sleepless night at home, Chloe met Rhodes in the bureau parking garage the following morning and they headed out in a bureau car. They left at six in the morning, making sure to beat the miserable Beltway traffic. Chloe noted that Rhodes was doing her best not to seem too pumped—it was a restraint that she masked poorly through long sips of coffee pretending to focus too hard on driving.

"It's okay," Chloe said. "You're going into this with me, so you can ask whatever questions you want." She shrugged as she merged onto the Beltway to make their way into Maryland. "I think you caught the gist of it in Johnson's office last night. Danielle is missing. It's really nothing too unusual … it's how she spent most of her teens and early twenties, just coming and going whenever she felt like it. But it's different this time because I have no idea where my Dad is, either."

"It makes sense that you'd assume the worst," Rhodes said. "Given everything you've been through over the last year. Which leads me to the obvious question: why didn't you just take a few personal days?"

"Because I would have ended up looking into the case. And I'd rather have a job with the bureau, actively working on a case and trusting the DC police to figure out where my sister is, rather than getting fired for not being able to stay out of the investigation during my so-called personal days."

"Damned if you do, damned if you don't," Rhodes sighed.

"Something like that."

"At the risk of pissing you off, I think Johnson is right, though. If not's in the bureau's jurisdiction, you have to just trust the cops."

"I know. It's harder than it sounds like when it's a sibling that's missing, though."

"I won't even try to pretend I know what that feels like," Rhodes said. The emotion in her voice was evident. It was clear she meant it.

"I appreciate that," Chloe said.

The whole exchange honestly only upset Chloe a bit more. It also made her wonder, though, if she was overreacting. Johnson had made it sound like it really wasn't too big of a deal and here Rhodes was, essentially agreeing with him.

They remained quiet for a while as Rhodes drove north. Just before they got into Baltimore, a slight drizzle of rain started to come down. They managed to sneak into the city just before the morning rush of traffic plagued the roads. Chloe looked through the scant information they had, just a few freshly printed pages in a folder Johnson had given them. The address of the most recent victim had been plugged into their GPS, a little subdivision about two miles outside of Baltimore proper.

"Fine, can you promise me something?" Rhodes asked as they closed in on the address.

"I don't make promises," Chloe said. She'd meant it as a joke but it came out rather harsh. "But I can do my best to keep my word."

"Okay, that'll have to do. I just need you to be honest with me and let me know if all the personal crap starts to wear on you while we're on this. For once, I'd like for you and I to just roll up on the scene and crack a case within twenty-four hours. No complications, no setbacks."

"Yes, *that* I can give you my word on."

This seemed to break the tension that had hovered in the car between them. By the time they entered the subdivision, Chloe felt almost normal. She was thinking of Danielle every few seconds, sure, but she was also recalling just how flippant Danielle had been in the past. When her past was considered, the fact that she was missing really wasn't all that strange.

True, but Dad, too?

She shut out the thought as Rhodes parked the car in front of a two-story house that was essentially a copy and paste job of every other house on the street. Not to say it wasn't gorgeous. It was simple but in a grand way, the sort of house seen in the *after* photos on all of those fixer-upper-type shows.

"Ready for this?" Rhodes asked.

Chloe bit back the sarcasm that crept up onto her tongue. If Rhodes was going to coddle her because of the Danielle situation, she wasn't sure she would be able to get through this case after all.

"Ready," was all she said as she stepped out of the car and into the sprinkling rain.

The detective who had been running the case was a lanky man named Anderson. He was sitting at the kitchen table when Chloe and Rhodes entered the house. He looked up to them from an iPad he was thumbing through, setting it aside apologetically as he got to his feet. Chloe took a peek at the screen as he stood and saw that he had been looking at crime scene photos from this very house.

"Ben Anderson," he said, offering his hand.

"Agents Fine and Rhodes," Chloe said, shaking his hand. "Been waiting long?"

"Just ten minutes or so. Of course, I've been here three or four times in the last sixteen hours, just trying to get a feel for the place."

"You were on the scene upon the discovery of the body?" Chloe asked.

"I was. Second on the scene."

"Where was the body located?" Rhodes asked.

Anderson waved them toward the back of the house as he picked up the iPad. He started walking across the kitchen, opening up a door that led outside. "Out here on the back porch... though there's nothing much to see."

They stepped out onto the back porch. Chloe could see nothing remotely of interest at first. It was a nice porch, looking out over about an acre of bright green back yard. A grill sat in the far corner, protected by a grill cover emblazoned with a Baltimore Ravens logo. The sparse patio furniture set up in the center of the porch was nice, but nothing special—likely from Wayfair or Costco. It was still drizzling out, leaving faint water drop marks on the wooden floor. Chloe noted a comma-shaped bloodstain on the boards—about the right size to partially encircle someone's head.

"The victim was Bo Luntz," Anderson said. "His wife, Sherry, discovered him when she got home from work. It was their anniversary. She found him out here, on the back porch, lying on the floor. She sort of blanked out for a while. She didn't even notice that a black sock had been shoved into his mouth, almost down his throat. She says she was vaguely aware of seeing it when she first spotted him, but... she was a mess, understandably."

"The blood," Chloe said, dropping down to her haunches. "It indicates that he wasn't just strangled. Was there evidence of a struggle?"

"No. Nothing was overturned, nothing out of the ordinary. The evidence came in a blow he suffered to the skull, right along the forehead."

That said, he handed Chloe the iPad he had been carrying. He had brought up a picture of the body. Chloe zoomed in on Bo Luntz's forehead. There was a definite indentation, and the beginnings of a bruise. From the shape of the indentation, she thought it might be something with a flat end, maybe five or six inches in width.

"The bruising looks fresh," Rhodes pointed out, looking over Chloe's shoulder. "How long after the body was discovered was this taken?"

"About an hour or so, I'd say. And based on what Mrs. Luntz told us, the blood was still wet when she found the body. So we figure he was killed within an hour or two of her coming home."

"No prints on the sock in his throat?" Chloe asked.

"None. No prints from inside, either. No signs of breaking and entering … nothing."

Rhodes started fishing through the files they had gotten from Johnson, shielding the papers from the rain by leaning the top half of her body forward. "Bo Luntz, fifty-two years of age, one child, employed by Mutual Telecom. No criminal record. Can you add anything to that, Detective Anderson?"

"Based on preliminary talks with neighbors and friends, all we know is that the guy was really well-liked. He was a volunteer firefighter, helped with charitable causes whenever he could. Was an assistant coach for a recreational football team. I interviewed five people myself and we got at least a dozen more on file. The guy was squeaky clean."

Chloe nodded, but she'd heard this kind of thing several times before. Most men could pull off looking squeaky clean on the surface. But she knew that once you did some digging, you found cracks in those clean surfaces, cracks that often led to grimy secrets.

"Any idea why a sock was shoved in his throat?" Chloe asked.

"No clue. We looked through his drawers upstairs, thinking we'd maybe find one that was missing its match, but not so much."

"Detective, can we get the name and number of the coroner that has the body?"

"Sure thing," he said, taking out his phone and automatically scrolling through his contacts for the information.

"And what about the first victim?" Chloe asked.

"His name was Richard Wells. He lives about twelve miles away, in the little town of Eastbrook. A neighborhood pretty similar to this one. Eastbrook PD is running with that case, but I have some of the details if you'd like them."

"Yes, please."

"Basically a carbon copy of what happened here. Wells was found dead in his bedroom, his head basically caved in, and a black sock in his mouth. Personality-wise, though, the two were quite different. Wells had been divorced last year. Rumors of a drinking problem. He worked as a private contractor, and his few employees were the only ones we could get information from. The ex-wife is already engaged again, living in Rhode Island. Both his parents are dead, no siblings...no one around that we could ask any sort of deep questions."

"So a dead end, more or less?" Rhodes asked.

"More or less," Anderson agreed.

Chloe looked back down at the boards that made up the porch floor. She studied the bloodstain, unable to shake the sight of the smear of blood she had seen on her father's teakettle. It sank into her and it felt like stepping out of a warm house and into a winter storm. And just like that, she was fairly certain she would not be able to shake it; Danielle's disappearance was going to haunt her until she heard from her, case or no case.

The worst part of all was that she was starting to resent Danielle for it, worrying that the mess of a woman her sister had once been was resurfacing.

If I find her, maybe I can prevent that, Chloe thought.

It was appealing, but as she continued to look at Bo Luntz's blood she knew that when it came to saving her sister, it was, much like saving Luntz's life, far too late.

In Chloe's experience, coroners came in one of two packages: quiet and almost morose in their work, or very excitable and maybe a little *too into* their work. The woman they met at the coroner's office that had been tasked with looking over Bo Luntz was the latter kind. Her name was Gerda Holloway and she looked like she belonged on one of those bachelor-type television shows rather than working with dead bodies. Even Chloe had to admit to herself just how good-looking the woman was, her hair in a ponytail, her eyes framed in librarian-style glasses as she greeted them in the lobby.

"Agents Rhodes and Fine," Rhodes said after Holloway had introduced herself.

"Come on back," Holloway said. "The body is prepped, but you're welcome to have a look before I start logging actual time."

They followed her out of the lobby and down a long corridor. When they came to the examination room where Luntz's body was being held, Holloway opened the door and held it for them with a smile, as if she was having a dinner party with friends rather than preparing to look over a murdered body.

They entered the room, Chloe taking a moment to adjust to the bright lights and sterile surfaces. Every time she walked into a coroner's examination room, she felt like she was walking into another world. But then she'd see the body on the table and she would come right back around to the real world.

It was the case now, with Bo Luntz. He was on the table, lifeless eyes closed. If not for the wound on his forehead, he would have looked normal. Holloway took a moment to let the agents get accustomed to the sight before stepping to the table with a tablet in her hand.

"As you can see, there was blunt force trauma to the skull," Holloway said. "There's no way to know for sure what it was, but given the angle, depth of the wound, and the way the skull seems to have collapsed, I'm banking on something as simple as a rock or as complex as some sort of concrete lawn decoration."

"Can we tell anything about the killer from any of that information?" Chloe asked.

"Well, as you can see, the angle of the wound seems to have a slight upward tilt to it. It's also the direction the force seems to push toward. There are many factors that could cause this, but it's safe bet the killer was shorter than the victim."

"According to the files," Rhodes said, "Bo Luntz was six-one. So lots of people would be shorter."

"Agreed," Holloway said. "However, if you look *very* close at the edge of the indentation along the skull, there is also evidence to suggest that it was not one single blow, but two. And the second one looks to have been a bit stronger, but it was a glancing blow."

Chloe approached the table and saw exactly what Holloway was talking about. Along the left side of the indentation in Luntz's forehead, the dent was about two inches deeper. The area also looked slightly darker, as if it had been hit with more force than the rest of the wound. Chloe cocked her head, trying to imagine if it was just a strangely shaped weapon that had caused it.

"My theory," Holloway said, "is that he was struck the first time and then a second immediately after, two quick successive blows. That explains the eerie aim, one blow right on top of the other. But because the second blow seems to have barely struck him, I'm assuming it came as he was falling."

"And both blows are right in the center of his head," Chloe noted. "If someone were to take him by surprise—sneaking up on him perhaps—such a perfectly placed blow would be unlikely, right?"

"Yes. Not impossible, mind you. But very unlikely."

"So it would be someone he probably knew was in the house?" Rhodes suggested.

"That's what I'd put my money on," Holloway said.

Chloe thought about the details Johnson had shared with them and the little bit Anderson had told them as well. No signs of forced entry, no indication of a struggle, and it occurred on their anniversary. Basic deduction and experience pointed to the wife.

"Did you find anything else in his throat other than the sock?" Chloe asked.

"No. But it was likely placed there after the fact. It seemed to have been placed with great care. The tongue was shoved back. Had it been put into his mouth while he was alive, the muscles of the tongue would have instantly pushed against it."

The inclusion of the sock made the whole thing weirder. It was the sort of oddity that Chloe usually got hung up on, as there was surely some sort of symbolism tied to it. And usually, there was motive wherever symbolism was found.

Chloe looked at the body a bit longer, trying to find anything else to point them in a direction other than the wife. When it was clear she was going to find nothing, she and Rhodes thanked Holloway before heading out.

"You thinking the wife, too?" Rhodes asked as they made their way back to the front of the building.

"I am. And if not as a potential suspect—which I believe she is right now—then to ask if she would have any idea why someone might shove a sock down his throat."

Rhodes nodded her agreement as they walked across the parking lot and got into the car. Before they were out of the lot, Chloe was on the phone with Detective Anderson, getting a location for Sherry Luntz. As she picked the phone up to place the call, she could not help the little spark of hope that reared its head, anticipating a missed call notification from Danielle.

Of course, there was no such thing, leaving Chloe no choice but to assume the worst and try to bury it all with the Luntz case.

CHAPTER SIX

Anderson seemed hesitant to send them over to speak with Sherry Luntz at first. According to police reports, she'd been emotionally affected to the point of blacking out twice after discovering the body. Chloe wasn't having any of it, though. She had dealt with grieving widows before, many of whom had been hiding secrets and unknowingly obstructing the progress of a case out of embarrassment.

"She's the only realistic suspect we have at this point," Chloe argued as they neared the Luntz residence. "With all due respect, you can tell us where she's staying or we can make calls back to DC and find out on our own."

Anderson finally bent and told them that Sherry was staying with her folks in the city. "But look," he said. "I can't overstress how broken this woman is. Could it just be one of you to speak with her?"

It wasn't the approach Chloe would typically take but she also knew it wasn't an argument worth having. Besides, if only one of them went to visit with Sherry Luntz, the other could canvass the Luntzes' street to see if the neighbors had any information to give.

This was how Chloe ended up arriving at the residence of Tamara Nelson, Sherry's sister, alone twenty minutes later. Rhodes had seemed quite content to speak to the neighbors while Chloe elected to speak to Sherry. While Chloe did not enjoy speaking to the recently bereaved, both she and Rhodes knew that she had a much stronger compassionate side than Rhodes. It was not something Rhodes seemed particularly proud of, but something she accepted.

Anderson had called ahead, letting Tamara know that an FBI agent was on the way. So when Chloe knocked on the door, it was answered almost right away. Both women were standing there to greet her, and it was easy to tell which was Sherry Luntz. She was the one who stood slightly behind her sister, her red hair in disarray, her skin pale except for the dark circles under her eyes. The eyes themselves were bloodshot from crying and though it looked like those eyes might slip closed at any moment, there was a lurking menace in them that made Chloe think this woman was not going to get much sleep anytime soon.

"Sherry Luntz?" Chloe asked.

The frazzled tired woman nodded, though she did not step forward. Her sister remained in front, as if protecting her.

"I'm Agent Fine. I believe Detective Anderson called to let you know I was coming?"

"He did," Tamara said. "Please don't take this the wrong way, but I'll be sitting in the room as you speak with Sherry."

"Of course," Chloe said. She was starting to wonder if Sherry was going to be talking at all. She looked absolutely wrecked—almost to the point of looking nearly comatose.

Tamara turned and walked inside without giving a proper invitation for Chloe to follow. Chloe did so anyway, closing the door behind her. Tamara led her into a beautifully decorated living room. A sweet smell wafted in from elsewhere in the house—some kind of tea, Chloe supposed.

"I understand how hard this must be for you, Mrs. Luntz," Chloe said. "I'll keep this as brief and painless as possible."

"No, it's fine," Sherry said. She had the voice of a woman who had just woken up from a twelve-hour sleep after a night of drinking. "I want to figure this out. Don't cut any corners for my sake."

Chloe glanced over to Tamara, as if for approval. The sister gave a shrug that seemed to have the weight of the world behind it.

"Mrs. Luntz, I know the details of the afternoon, so I can skip over some of that. What I need to know about are the in-the-weeds type things about your husband's life. Were there people you might consider his enemies, or just people you feel might not have liked him?"

"I've thought so hard about that, trying to figure it out," she said. "The only person I could come up with was an old business rival, but he lives out in California somewhere. I know it sounds like I'm just praising my dead husband but really, everyone liked Bo."

"Had he mentioned any hardships at work recently?"

"None. Nothing. I even had Tamara call his boss to see if there might be something he was hiding, but there was nothing."

"You have a child together, right?" Chloe asked.

"Yes, a son. Luke. He started college this year. He's here, too. Sleeping, back in the guest bedroom. He's sort of…just blank right now."

"Have you asked him these same questions?" Chloe asked.

"Not in such a blunt way, but yes. We've tried to figure out who might have done it. I feel like it might be one of those random home invasions, but… nothing was missing. Nothing was taken."

"I called the credit card companies for Sherry yesterday," Tamara said. "All of the cards were still in Bo's wallet, but I figure maybe there was some sort of digital fraud going on or something. But everything seemed okay. If it was some random sociopath that did this, it was just for the taking of a life."

"I checked and checked last night, Luke and I," Sherry said. "We couldn't find anything missing."

Chloe knew what she wanted to ask next, but it was going to be a tough question to get out. Already, she was getting a very good impression that Sherry had absolutely nothing to do with her husband's murder. You could fake crying, you could even fake a breakdown. But blacking out from grief in the presence of the police and missing enough sleep to make her look like an extra in a zombie film… that was genuine stuff.

"What about anything in the house or even the yard or back porch that might have been misplaced? Maybe something that looked like it had been moved just a few inches or so?" she asked.

This was her way of asking if they might have inadvertently found the object that was used to attack Bo.

"Nothing we noticed."

"Can you think of anyone who might have a key to get into your home?"

"No one. We've never had any need to give a key out. We've never had a maid or cleaning lady, never had family stay over. Nothing like that."

"And what about security systems? I saw none when my partner and I visited the home."

"Nope. We kept saying we were going to invest in one, but the neighborhood is so safe…it's just something we kept putting off and never getting around to."

"One more thing, Mrs. Luntz…and I'm sorry but it might be difficult."

"It's okay."

"One very odd detail about your husband's body was—"

"The sock in his mouth," she said. She said it was if she were giving the punchline to a weird joke…like she knew it was coming.

"Yes. Any idea what it might mean?"

"Absolutely no idea," Sherry said, her voice wavering on tears. "When I found him like that, I knew there was something in his mouth, but I didn't know what it was. I never knew what it was until hours later when I remembered it and asked. Detective Anderson told me it was a sock. When I heard that, I thought I was maybe still blacked out and having some weird dream but…no. That's what it was. He even showed me a picture of it last night, after it…well, after the medical examiner…"

"It's okay," Chloe said. "We can stop, Mrs. Luntz."

"I don't know if it helps in any way or not," Sherry said, "but it wasn't one of his socks. He hated those thick black socks, even in winter. His feet tended to sweat and those thick black ones made him miserable." The ghost of a smile touched her lips as she thought about this personal pet peeve.

Chloe reached into her jacket pocket and removed one of her business cards. She handed it to Tamara, not wanting to give any added pressures or responsibilities to Sherry. "Please ... if either of you think of anything else, no matter how small, call me."

"Of course," Tamara said. She barely looked at Chloe, though. She was focused on her sister, gauging her strength. After an awkward silence, Tamara got to her feet to take Chloe back to the door.

Tamara walked out onto the porch with her, closing the door behind them. She folded her arms against her chest and looked almost apologetically at Chloe.

"She's not just painting a pretty picture," Tamara said. "Bo was one of the good guys, you know? Humble, kind, loved his wife and son. I don't think I've ever heard anyone say a cross word about him—not even our mother, and that's saying something."

"I'm beginning to understand that about him. I do have one thing I'd like to ask you ... and it's strictly for formalities' sake."

"If I think Sherry might have done it?"

Chloe frowned and nodded. "I am all but certain she didn't, but I need to hear it from someone who knows her as a matter of record."

"There's no way Sherry did it. And even if I thought she might have even been thinking about something like that, you can check with her work. The police already did, though. They have her on security camera leaving the building at five-oh-two that afternoon. Given the time they think he was killed ... there's no way it would have been her."

Chloe almost decided to push a bit, to ask if there were any skeletons in Bo's closet. But she not only felt that she would get nothing out of Tamara, but also that doing so would only upset her. And for right now, she seemed to have a grieving wife and a supportive sister who could potentially come in handy for information later down the road.

"Thank you for your time," Chloe said. "And really ... even the smallest thing, let me know."

"We will."

Chloe hurried down the porch and back to her car, hoping Rhodes had come across something. Rhodes had a way of pushing without coming off as rude and if she was questioning only neighbors without deep emotional ties, perhaps she'd had more luck. Chloe drove back out toward the Luntzes' neighborhood, the drizzling rain still sprinkling down and casting a gray hue to the day.

Chloe was not one to believe in omens or superstitions, but she could not help but feel that the rain—which seemed to be escalating a bit as it came down—might be a sign of things to come.

CHAPTER SEVEN

Rhodes seemed to be in a good mood as Chloe picked her up. If she was irritated with anything it was that she was slightly wet from the rain as she got into the passenger seat. Chloe started driving down the street right away, even before they compared notes. She wanted to get out of the rain, maybe into a diner or coffee shop. There, they could compare notes and come up with the best course to take from here.

"Any luck?" she asked as they came to the end of the Luntzes' street and to the grander sweep of the neighborhood's central thoroughfare.

"Well, I'm discovering that there might as well be some sort of Bo Luntz fan club around here," Rhodes said. "Not only does everyone like him, but a few people even expressed regret over not getting to know him better."

"How many were you able to speak with?"

"I canvassed the street; most were at work, of course, but I did manage to talk with four different people, in three different homes. They all spoke highly of him. An older woman in one of the last three houses up from the Luntz residence said Bo let her borrow his car for three weeks after she wrecked hers and her insurance company jerked her around. No questions asked, and he barely knew her."

"And no one heard or saw anything?" Chloe asked.

"Nothing."

Seems to be a running theme lately, Chloe said, thinking of how easily Danielle and her father had simply disappeared.

They both ruminated over this until they came to a simple little diner several miles up the road, a wannabe hipster coffee house that was built around the fact they specialized in gluten-free muffins. They had been working together long enough to be comfortable in the process of entering a place, placing their orders, going to the restroom, and then meeting at a table to go over the case notes. Chloe was slightly amazed sometimes at how far they had come. It seemed like just yesterday that Rhodes had seemed almost miffed that she had been stuck with Chloe as a partner. That had, of course, been before Chloe had saved her life after she'd been shot on their first case together.

Chloe sipped from her black coffee while Rhodes took a gulp from her chai tea latte. Together, they started diving into the notes, comparing and contrasting, adding in the fact that neighbors and family alike had offered nothing new this morning.

The one new certainty that Chloe had to offer seemed like a strong one, but it was hard for her to say it simply. "I feel like the wife can be ruled out. Her sister says the police checked with her work and they have her leaving the building at five-oh-two. The times just don't line up."

Rhodes nodded, flipping through the little bit of paperwork they had on the case. "They're estimating that he was killed between three thirty and four forty-five. People at Bo's office report seeing him there, in the office, as late as three thirty. According to one of his co-workers, Bo had mentioned leaving early to do something special for his anniversary."

"That's odd. It makes it seem like the killer knew he was leaving—that he'd be home early."

"That, or the killer was already there for some other reason and killed Bo out of shock and surprise."

They let this sink in for a moment. Chloe looked outside at the rain, coming down steadier now. "Sherry Luntz says no one outside of her or Bo had a key to the house. No family members, no cleaning lady, no trusted friends, nothing."

"And no signs of a break-in ..."

Chloe knew where she wanted to go with her hunches. It was the obvious place but, for some reason, didn't quite feel right. Still, she said it anyway. "So, Bo let the person in. More than that, maybe they arrived at the house with him."

"An affair, maybe?"

"You said it, not me. But … if he was planning something for his anniversary that afternoon, that seems sort of ballsy, right?"

"Or stupid," Rhodes said.

"And you know, there's something else that just now occurred to me. Everything we know about the murder of the first victim, Richard Wells, is a carbon copy of Bo Luntz's. Sock in the mouth, bludgeoned about the head. And they were only two days apart. So if you do the math …"

"If you do the math," Rhodes picked up, "and this is a serial killer rather than isolated yet connected incidents, there could be another victim in the next twenty-four hours."

"Maybe we're to the point now where we stop digging deeper into Luntz and see what we can dig up on victim number one."

"Yeah, but Anderson said there was no one around here that he was close to," Rhodes pointed out. "No family, no friends, no one."

"Exactly," Chloe said, getting to her feet. "If you ask me, that sounds like the exact sort of man who would be great at keeping secrets."

They called ahead on their way to Eastbrook. Because it was such a small town with a limited police force, a helpful woman in the records department was able to simply email over digital copies of the case files rather than having Chloe and Rhodes meet up with an officer. As far as Chloe was concerned, this was great news. She much preferred to work a case without the aid of local police. Yes, they were often very helpful but they also tended to be instantly sympathetic with basically any victim from their neck of the woods.

They were four miles away from Eastbrook by the time the files had come through. Rhodes read through them as Chloe drove. The rain was letting up, the sun starting to peek through the scattering rain clouds. Little clouds of mist rose from the road ahead of them.

"Richard Wells, age fifty-two, resident of Eastbrook for most of his adult life. His record is very brief—two DUIs and one failure to appear in court. License was suspended three years ago as a result. Local PD have reached out to his ex-wife and, while helpful with their questions, she did not seem all that upset about the murder. She's the only number listed as any sort of emergency contact or next of kin."

"And she's in Rhode Island, right?"

"Right."

"Wells was a private contractor, correct? We have a company name?"

"Yeah, and not a creative one. Wells Construction and Design, located in Eastbrook."

Chloe was about to ask Rhodes to plug it into the GPS but Rhodes was already on it. It made her think of how Johnson had assured them that one reason he gave them the case was because he felt it would be a good fit for them. She assumed she and Rhodes were developing as a unit more so than any other of the other agents who had come out of their class at the academy. When they got on these borderline-psychic frequencies with one another, it was easy to believe.

When they arrived at the small office space that was Wells Construction and Design, it was shortly after 11 o'clock. The office was located on what served as Main Street in Eastbrook, a town that Chloe assumed only existed at all because it was in such close proximity to Baltimore. It was the sort of town people might stop by if they needed to gas up or grab a snack before finishing the drive into the city.

Chloe parked in front of the building, worried that it might actually be closed due to the death of the owner. She found the front door unlocked, though. The office consisted of one large primary space that had been divided up with cubicle walls. One large desk sat in the front, positioned in an L-shape so the woman behind it could greet people as they came in the door.

She looked up at Chloe and Rhodes now, her eyes indicating that she was quite bored. Chloe imagined it must be strange for a small business to try carrying on once the namesake of said company had been so brutally murdered.

"Can I help you ladies?" the woman asked.

"Yes, actually," Chloe said. She ran through introductions, both she and Rhodes showing their IDs. "We're looking into the murder of Richard Wells. He has no family around here, and it seems the people he was closest to might have been those who worked for him."

"That's true," she said. "It's a shame, too. You don't really realize such a thing about someone until after they're gone, you know?"

"Can you tell me if the company plans to go on without him?"

The woman shrugged, a nonchalant gesture that made it seem as if not only did she not know, but she did not care. "We're waiting for his lawyers to figure that one out. Richard apparently did not have a will. So the company wasn't left to anyone. We've got three builders that work here and they are all out at two different construction sites right now, doing their best to finish up some projects before the shit hits the legal fan."

"Do you mind if I get your name?" Chloe asked.

"Sure. It's Patty Marsh."

"Ms. Marsh, have you been working here long?"

"Six years now."

"And what was your overall impression of Richard Wells? Not just as a boss, but a human being?"

"Well, he was hardworking, that's for sure. But I think he's one of those guys who peaked in high school and sort of relived that, you know? He was a heavy drinker, a big flirt even though he was married up until six months back. He was the type that always managed to tell some story about his glory days playing high school football, you know? It was sad, really, but it made him happy."

"Did he ever snap at you or the other workers?"

"Oh, I'm sure he broke on the builders here and there. But they were all good friends. Those guys are a bit younger than Richard but were sort of the same story…not much going in in their lives, resorting back to tales of high school and college to make themselves feel good. God…this makes me sound like a bitch."

"Not at all," Rhodes said. "I wonder, given the nature of his job, if Richard ever made any enemies? Maybe unhappy customers?"

"The cops asked us the same thing and we couldn't come up with anything. Sure, Richard had his demons, but he was a hard worker. He drank a lot and really didn't make much of a secret about it. But he somehow balanced that and his work life. He took great pride in his work. I don't think there's ever been a cross customer to deal with ever since I've been working here."

"When do you expect the builders back?" Chloe asked.

"Not until the end of the day. But at the risk of sounding rude, they're going to tell you the exact same stuff I just did."

"All the same, maybe we should have access to speak with them, just in case."

"Sure thing," Patty said. She opened her drawer and rifled around through a series of business cards. She handed three cards to Chloe—one for each of the workers—and that ended the visit.

Chloe looked over each of the cards as they got back into the car. She pocketed them as Rhodes got into the passenger seat. She already had her phone out, pulling up her Recently Called list. Chloe grinned, assuming she was thinking the same thing she was: that they needed to check out Richard Wells's house, and they'd need Detective Anderson's assistance at getting inside.

As Chloe pulled back out onto the street, she was proven correct when she heard Rhodes say: "Detective Anderson, it's Agent Rhodes. Are you available to help us get into Richard Wells's house?"

Feeling encouraged that she and Rhodes were so well-synced, Chloe drove on, managing to find the first stirring of excitement about the case. Danielle was still there in the forefront of her mind, but it was shrinking slightly by the minute.

CHAPTER EIGHT

Eastbrook was a strange little town. While the town's central hub consisted of only two or three streets of businesses, the rest of the town proper was made up of several subdivisions. Many of them were built on beautiful wooden lots with spacious yards while a few others were really nothing more than overpriced homes piled on top of one another.

The latter was the kind of house that Richard Wells had lived in. It was a nice home—a two-story that Chloe couldn't see held any one single style, but incorporated several. The neighborhood was much like the one Sherry and Bo Luntz had lived in, though the houses were much closer together. As Chloe and Rhodes made their way to the front door, Chloe glanced to the small yard and estimated there might be half an acre all told.

Anderson had informed them that all they needed to enter the house was the security code for the front door, which he gave them. Rhodes punched in the five-digit code and they stepped inside without any problem.

Wells's house was a bit smaller than the Luntzes', the downstairs completely open and revealing only a large living space, a kitchen and dining room combo, and a single bathroom. From the looks of it, the place had been in need to tidying up when Wells had been killed. There were a few empty beer bottles on the coffee table in the living room, a pair of dirty work boots on the floor right beside the couch, and a pile of dirty dishes overflowing in the sink.

"According to the forensics report," Rhodes said, reading from her iPad, "his body was discovered by a drinking buddy, a guy named Al Sawyer. Sawyer has been cleared of the murder because there are at least a dozen people who helped back up his alibis for the few days before the murder. He's currently at Baltimore Central Booking and Intake for causing an accident the night of Richard's murder. Charged with a DWI...his third, so he's looking at some time."

"He gave a statement, right?"

"Yeah. He found Richard upstairs, half in and half out of his bedroom. Blood on the floor, a massive wound on the side of his head. Coroner's report says the wound was caused by blunt force trauma."

She showed Chloe a picture of the wound. It was quite grisly, but it was easy to tell that whatever had been used to strike Richard Wells in the head was not the same thing used on Bo Luntz.

A brief image of Danielle flashed through her mind. She wondered where she might be right now if she had found something like this in her father's townhouse...Danielle, bludgeoned in such a way.

She shook the thought off and focused on her work. She hated that it was so hard to do. And she hated Johnson even more for putting her in this position.

"Sock in the mouth, too," Chloe said, pointing to the picture and coming back around as if her thoughts had not derailed there for a second.

They'd already known all of this, but to see the imagery while standing in the man's house made it all feel new—a little more urgent.

They walked upstairs to the bedroom, Chloe taking note of some of the features of the home as she went. There were three pictures in frames, one beside the other, on the way up the stairs. One was obviously quite old, a picture of a man dressed in hunting gear, posted by the back of a pickup truck. The second was of a teenage girl at high school graduation, cheesing big-time at the camera. The third was of what looked like a JV football team, the players no older than twelve or thirteen years of age. She couldn't be sure, but she thought the photo wasn't very recent; it wasn't nearly as faded as the one with the hunting fellow, but it had a sort of hazy quality to it.

"We know if Wells had kids?" Chloe asked.

"Two daughters. They both left with the mother. One is twenty years old, about to finish college. The other is fifteen."

When they came to the bedroom, the blood stain on the carpet was impossible to miss. It was just inside the opened bedroom door. There were light splatters of it on the door itself but the vast majority of it was contained in two large misshapen circles on the carpet. They carefully stepped over the stains and into the bedroom.

The bed was unmade, there were a few dirty articles of clothing in the floor, and there was a small stack of paperwork on the floor by the bed. Chloe checked the papers and saw that they consisted of two contracts for future jobs for Wells Construction and Design— jobs that would now likely never come to pass.

As Rhodes broke off and checked the adjoining bathroom, Chloe walked over to the nightstand. The only things worth a second look on it were a cell phone bill, a copy of *Sports Illustrated,* and a bottle of NyQuil. She then went to his dresser on the other side of the room, where a few other things sat.

Beside the small oscillating fan, she found a framed picture that had been laid down on its back. She picked it up and saw a picture of a married couple on their wedding day. She had only seen Richard Wells in the files—so, in other words, dead and in pictures—but she recognized the face as his. She knew he had only been married once, so that made the woman in the white dress beside him the current ex-wife who had moved to Rhode Island.

There was another picture under the wedding photo, this one not in a frame. Chloe picked it up and for a moment, some traitorous emotion welled up inside of her. She felt a lump forming in her throat and the beginnings of tears in her eyes.

The photo showed a man—Richard Wells from about ten years ago, she estimated—standing with two young girls. Even someone not looking for links or clues could tell that these were Richard's daughters. The resemblance in the face of the youngest one was uncanny.

Her emotion came from this eerie resemblance. The similarities between Richard and his youngest daughter was just as strong as the one Danielle had shared with their own father. And just like that, Danielle's shadow loomed over everything else in her mind. It encompassed everything, making her feel guilty for not doing more to find her, making her feel sad because she knew in her gut that Danielle was in danger.

I should be out looking for her, Chloe thought. *Not the DC cops…*

"What you got there?"

Rhodes was approaching from the bathroom, giving Chloe a wary look.

"A few pictures. This one looks to be about ten years old if I had to guess. Wells and his daughters."

Rhodes looked at it, and then the wedding picture. "Looks like a normal happy family on the surface, huh?"

"Most do," Chloe quipped.

Rhodes set the pictures back on top of the dresser and took a moment, as if trying to carefully select what she was about to say. In the end, she came out with a simple: "You okay, Fine?"

"No, I'm not." Then, in a move that alarmed not only Rhodes but Chloe herself, Chloe swiped the photos from the dresser. The framed one clattered to the floor while the other fluttered like some dead and dramatic fly.

"Chloe…"

Chloe raised her hand and walked out of the room. "Just give me a fucking minute, okay?"

She stepped over Richard Wells's bloodstain and back out into the hallway. As she walked down the stairs, doing her best to stave off what felt like a miniature panic attack, she again spied the pictures on the wall. The wife was not in any of them, but he'd kept one in a frame upstairs. She knew enough about grief to know what this meant: Wells had not been ready to move on from his wife, but did not want any visitors to his home to know it. Chloe imagined Wells kept the picture in his room to stare at on the nights when he truly missed her the most.

It was a thought that did nothing to help with the case, but it did help to push the topic of Danielle's disappearance away. She hated herself for having to distance herself from Danielle but she knew if she didn't get a handle on it soon, she was going to become an obstacle to this case.

But where the hell is she? What's she doing? And how is my miserable father involved?

It occurred to her that Danielle might be dead already—that their father had not changed at all and had been trying to lead them both astray this entire time.

No, Danielle is smarter than that…

And there it was again, Danielle's disappearance ruling over everything else in her head.

This time, the tears did come. She wiped them away quickly, realizing that having an emotional breakdown in the house of a man who had recently been murdered had to be one of the most depressing things she had ever heard of. It was almost morbidly funny in a way.

She heard footsteps behind her. When she turned, she saw Rhodes coming down the stairs. She, too, was looking at the pictures on the wall: the hunting man, the JV football team, one of Wells's daughters at graduation.

"I found a scrap of paper on the dresser," Rhodes said. "You knocking the pictures off uncovered it."

"Rhodes, I'm sorry…I'm having a hard time with the whole Danielle thing and…"

Rhodes shook her head. "Don't apologize. Just…let's do what we can for now. I know Anderson said the wife was basically uncooperative, but we need to talk to her."

"I agree. Maybe we can get the number from Anderson."

"No need," she said, handing Chloe the scrap of paper she had brought down.

Chloe took it and saw that there was a name at the top of the scrap: Angie. The name was followed by a phone number.

"I googled the area code," Rhodes said. "It's Providence, Rhode Island."

"You want to do the honors?" Chloe asked.

Rhodes didn't answer right away. Chloe knew what she was doing; she was waiting to make sure Chloe was ready to take this next step. Chloe adored her for taking the precaution but wished the hard-ass version of Rhodes she had originally met would come through from time to time.

"Sure," Rhodes said, taking out her cell phone. "I'd be happy to."

She punched in the numbers, placed the phone on speaker mode, and then set it on Richard Wells' coffee table.

As the phone began to ring, Chloe felt her heart do a little back-flip in her chest. At any moment, she was expecting the ringing of that phone to stop and provide them with nothing more than a series of clicks—the exact result she'd gotten every time she'd tried to call Danielle over the course of the last two days.

When the phone was answered by the woman who had at one time called this very house her home, that negativity was dashed. It brought Chloe back into the present, where Danielle might still be missing, but there was still a killer to find.

It took Chloe a moment to realize that the voice speaking to them was telling them to leave a message. She also noted that Angie Wells had apparently not gotten her name changed yet.

"This is Angie Wells," the woman's voice said. "Leave me a message and I'll return your call. Thanks!"

Chloe did exactly that, keeping her message short and sweet— but also including that the call was from the FBI and needed to be returned as soon as possible.

Rhodes ended the call and pocketed her cell phone. "I don't know about you," she said, "but I'm about ready to get out of here. Want to go see if Anderson has anywhere for us to set up a little workspace? I need a whiteboard ... some coffee ..."

Chloe nodded in agreement. She had another apology on her tongue but swallowed it down. It would only be embarrassing for her *and* Rhodes. They left the house and when Chloe pulled the door shut behind her, she did not hear the usual mechanical click or subtle beep most electronic lock systems made once the lock was reengaged. She made a mental note of it, but had nearly forgotten it by the time she was back behind the wheel.

CHAPTER NINE

Danielle again found herself wondering if she had, over the course of her harder years, become some sort of a monster without realizing it. She supposed it was possible, and it was very easy to imagine as she sat on her little seat of wooden pallets and looked at her father.

He was still bound from the ceiling, still gagged. He winced every now and then. She assumed it was because his arms were surely getting sore being stretched up like that.

Seeing him like that, she did not feel sorry for him, which made her wonder if she was indeed a monster.

However, she figured she could be more civil about this. The whole hang-him-by-his-arms-from-the-ceiling approach was a little much. But she wasn't sure how else to get hm to stay put. She'd thought about tying him to her little seat of pallets, but did not trust herself to make the knots tight enough. Plus, it would make it easier for him to escape.

"Mmnfff."

He'd been making this sound for about fifteen minutes now. She wondered if he wanted some more water. Slowly, she got off of her pallet-seat and grabbed up the bottle and carried it over to him.

She untied the makeshift gag and offered him the water. He opened his mouth for it, took a mouthful, and then nodded. She took the bottle away and stepped back, leaving the gag off for the time being.

"The diary says everything I need to know," Danielle said. "I just need to hear you say it. I need to hear you confess it."

"I have nothing to confess."

This was perhaps the most irritating thing of all. He did not know she had the voice recorder. It was the digital kind that could run for hours. She had clicked it on before getting up to get the water, hoping this would be the moment he fessed up. The fact that he had no idea she had the recorder and *still* wasn't confessing was placing far too many doubts in her head.

"Do I need to read more of the diary to you? Did you enjoy hearing the ways you terrorized her?"

"Danielle, I—"

She did not interrupt; she was curious to see what he had to say. But apparently, there was nothing. She shook her head at him and reached for the gag again.

"Danielle, this is lunacy," he said. "Do you have any idea the amount of trouble you could get in for this?"

"You think I'm worried about that? If you'd been a better father, you might know that I'm not especially worried about getting in trouble." She stepped up to him, their noses nearly touching, and sneered at him. "But you were never there. Never. God...I hope being an absolute selfish shithead was worth it. I hope you enjoyed that time in prison, thinking of Ruthanne Carwile while your daughters were raised by their grandparents. I hope it was worth it."

"Danielle, I always thought of you girls. Always. I love you both so much..."

"Then prove it."

"How?" he asked, starting to break down into tears.

"Confess. Tell me everything...tell me how my mother *really* died."

He looked away from her, lost in a bout of hitching sobs.

He was pathetic. It took everything in her not to smash him across the face with her fist. She clenched her hand into a fist, fully prepared to do it, but stopped at the last second. Instead, she reached out for the gag and placed it over his mouth again. He whined against it, opening his tear-streaked eyes and pleading with her through his stare.

"We can try again later," she said. "We're in the middle of nowhere, Dad. I've got nothing but time."

She returned to the pallets and turned her back to him so he would not see her turning off the digital recorder. She then sat back down and picked up the diary. She did not read from it again, but held on to it as a reminder. She held on to it and looked at her father, wondering if she would be able to kill him if it came down to it.

She felt the weight of the diary in her hands and decided that she could. Her mother's life beyond the age of thirty-six had been totally annihilated by this man—this selfish and deplorable man.

Danielle squeezed the journal tighter, as if anchoring herself to her hatred of him.

Yeah, she thought. *I think I could kill him if I wanted. And I think, before it's all said and done, I will.*

CHAPTER TEN

Gordon Nettle had been thinking about high school a lot over the past few days. It was weird, because he had put those years behind him as soon as he could. It wasn't that Gordon had hated high school per se, but it had been a big letdown. He'd attended two years of community college straight out of high school, had found an okay job as an assistant manager at a small marketing company, and that had been that. High school had been pushed back to the farthest corners of his mind: the rejections from girls, the struggles to maintain honor roll so his parents wouldn't lay into him. He was glad he'd never felt the need to hang onto it.

But here he was, sitting on his couch, staring blankly at the TV on a Thursday afternoon, and thinking of high school—chiefly because of the news he'd hear about Bo Luntz. He'd known Bo quite well in high school and, upon finding that they only lived about forty minutes away from one another, had been trying to schedule a time to get together for some wings and beer. But they had put it off for more than two years, usually because of busy schedules. But now Bo was dead…and while he mourned the loss of a man he once called a friend back in high school, he felt no real loss.

No, he was thinking about Bo so much because of the way he had died. The man had not just died; he'd been murdered. Bludgeoned in the head with a black sock stuffed deep into his mouth. It was the first time in his life someone he knew had been murdered. More than that, it had been in such a strange way.

It was the strangeness that had Gordon so hung up on the act. It had him thinking of Bo back in high school. They'd been decent friends—not best friends by any means, but they'd hung out quite a bit. Unless something drastic had occurred in Bo's life after high school, Gordon could not imagine anyone wanting to kill the young man he had once known.

It was the inclusion of the black sock that Gordon was hung up on. It stuck in his head like a bad record, skipping a thread and repeating the same two or three words over and over again. It made no real sense, though he knew it should.

You know why, some sickened part of him thought. *You just buried it deep, didn't you?*

Yes, he had. They all had.

Gordon checked the time and saw that it was 5:20. His wife was going to be late tonight, as she was heading out for her usual Thursday afternoon cocktail with friends from work. He had at least another two hours of doing absolutely nothing. He scrolled through Facebook for a while, seeing that a few other people he followed from his high school years had shared the link to the same story he had already read about Bo Luntz.

After a while, it was just too much. He tossed his phone to the other end of the couch, replaced it with the TV remote, and cued up ESPN. It was baseball season, which he cared virtually nothing about, but he figured he could maybe catch a few tidbits on the upcoming NFL preseason games.

He sat there for fifteen minutes, sipping from a bottle of beer he'd opened the moment he got home. It was rare that he got to just sit and chill. It made him feel a little tired, his thoughts again drifting back to high school and—

He snapped out of his little zone-out when he heard a shuffling noise from the back of the house. It had come from the other side of the kitchen, somewhere in the dining room. He knew the sound right away because he'd heard it countless times. The vertical blinds on the sliding patio door were being shuffled.

But that was odd; they only moved when someone opened or closed the patio door.

Curious, he got up from the couch and walked through the kitchen. From the back of the kitchen, he could see the patio door.

It was closed, but the blinds were trembling a bit. He walked into the dining room and looked around. The dining room sat at the back of the house, connected to the foyer by the front door and the kitchen. From there, he could see most of the kitchen and very little of the living room. From where he stood, he could barely see the glow of the TV.

He peered through the blinds and onto the back porch. There was no one and nothing there, nor in the back yard.

Weird, he thought.

It wasn't enough to make him panic, though. He was sure there could be any number of reasons the blinds could have been disturbed. There could have been …

From behind him, a footstep.

He turned, confused but expecting to see his wife.

But the face he saw, though familiar, was not that of his wife. He was too confused and startled to understand the severity of the situation. Yes, he recognized the face. But by the time he made the connection and knew who it was, they were bringing their right arm forward at a blinding speed. There was something in that hand, something gray and—

He was struck in the head, the right side of his face going numb as a hollow pounding noise rattled his head. Pain exploded, his skull a chorus of pain.

Gordon stumbled backward, bumping into the patio door and causing the blinds to clatter against the glass. As he rebounded from it, still dazed and letting out a moan of pain, the familiar face was there again. Another punch came, and then another.

Gordon wasn't sure how many there were. He counted at least four before he was on the floor and staring up at a ceiling that had suddenly seemed to turn a weird shade of gray.

Then that familiar face was there again, looking down at him.

Hey, I know you … he thought dreamily.

And then he saw what they held in the other hand.

A black sock.

Just before Gordon felt the cotton of the sock against his lips and tongue, it dawned on his pain-riddled mind why the image of a black sock had stuck with him when he had learned about Bo Luntz's death.

But the thought was fleeting and, as it turned out, was the last thing on Gordon Nettles's mind before the gray ceiling overhead turned black, just like everything else around him.

CHAPTER ELEVEN

One of the things Chloe was beginning to learn about Agent Rhodes was that when she was given a whiteboard and enough time, she could often create something pretty close to magic. For Chloe, her strength had always been examining a crime scene and stepping into the killer's point of view. But for Rhodes, she excelled when she could map things out logically, armed with case notes and a whiteboard.

Chloe watched Rhodes at work while she sat behind a desk in one of the spare rooms in the Baltimore Police Department's Central District Headquarters. Anderson had acquired the room for them and had asked to be notified if they needed any help whatsoever. Chloe almost wished they'd opted for the much smaller police department in Eastbrook, but there was something to be said for a busy police department with a huge well of resources to draw from.

Or, in Rhodes's case, a whiteboard and some dry-erase markers. She'd spent a good half an hour jotting down ideas and possible connections on it. Chloe had helped as needed, doing her own digging through the case files only to come up with nothing.

Her findings had been added to Rhodes's on the board and as she looked at it now, she realized just how deeply at the bottom of this case they were.

"Connections," Rhodes said, leaning back against the table and looking at her work. She fiddled nervously with the marker she had used while she read over it all. "Both victims were fifty-two years of age. Both married, both with kids that had moved away from home. Both were home alone in the afternoon when the murders happened."

She stopped here, sighed, and tossed the marker lazily up onto the board. "And that's where the similarities and connections end."

"Well, maybe there's more to be found in their differences than their similarities," Chloe pointed out. She looked to the right side of the board where Rhodes had written down the many differences between the two. Some were rather subtle while others were very much in-your-face.

"Wells went to trade school, while Luntz went to college. Luntz seemed to be a stable husband and good father while Wells seems to be the exact opposite. While they both *have* lived either in Baltimore or a surrounding area for all of their lives, it appears that they attended different high schools."

"Ah, one more connection for you, though," Rhodes said. "That black sock. What the hell? I feel like it's the killer rubbing something in their faces—no pun intended. It's got to mean something."

They both looked back to the whiteboard, Chloe waiting for *something* to leap out at them. Before Chloe could get her head back into that space, though, Rhodes's phone rang. She checked it and then looked at Chloe with a bit of excitement on her face.

"It's Angie Wells," Rhodes said.

Rhodes sat down, placing her phone in the center of the table. She answered the call, putting it on speaker mode.

"This is Agent Rhodes," she said.

"Hi," a woman's voice said, already sounding nervous and uncertain. "This is Angie Wells. I had a message from you, saying you need to speak to me urgently."

"Yes, that's right, and thanks for calling back. You should also know that my partner, Agent Fine, is here with me as well. We were hoping you could answer some questions for us regarding Richard's murder."

"I can," she said. "But I've already told the police everything I know. And I'm sort of in a hurry. I'm about to get on a plane to come down there ... I need to meet my kids for the funeral tomorrow."

"I appreciate that, but being that it's a bureau matter, we need to sort of start from scratch here. But of course, we will be very respectful of your time."

"Why is the FBI on the case now?" Angie asked.

"Because there's been a second murder. It was the same set-up as before ... the same set-up as Richard. And typically, similarities like we're seeing here mean there could very well be more on the way."

"When was this other one murdered?" Angie asked.

"Two days ago. Just outside of Baltimore."

"My God." She paused for a moment before saying, in a rather light and out of breath manner: "So what do you need to know?"

"Well," Chloe said, "we already spoke to a woman he worked with and learned basically the same things you told the police: no enemies, no bad blood with anyone. So what can you tell us about Richard? About your marriage in particular?"

"Well, Richard and I were high school sweethearts, but I think we sort of fell out of that crazy teenage sorta love at least ten years ago. Sort of just going through the motions because of our daughters. We started arguing a lot, started growing apart. I put my newfound energy into our daughters and my job. Richard put his into drinking."

"Was there ever any kind of abuse?" Rhodes asked.

"No. He was absent most of the time emotionally, but Richard was a pussycat. He would never hurt anyone like that."

"During his drinking spells, he never came home griping about any run-ins at the bars? Never complained about people he was working for?"

"No. I thought long and hard about it after I spoke with the cops, and I can't think of a single thing."

"Ms. Wells ... did the black sock found in Richard's mouth have any meaning to you?"

"No," she said. "I found it odd and sort of degrading. There's no love lost between Richard and I, but even I found that deplorable. That's the thing I kept getting hung up on after they told me what had happened—the one thing that actually made me cry. But ... Jesus, I guess you guys think I'm a terrible woman, huh?"

"We're not investigating your marriage," Chloe pointed out. "But tell us ... did you know Bo Luntz at all?"

"Bo ... yeah. Honestly, I probably haven't thought of him in years, but yeah. Why do you ... wait. Is he the second one?"

"Yes, I'm afraid he is. Mrs. Wells, how exactly did you know him?"

"Well, I hadn't spoken to him in ages. God ... probably not since a few years after high school."

"Did you go to high school with him?" Chloe asked, starting to sniff out a connection.

"No. We were in grade school together but then he moved out of the city, I think. Up until fifth grade or so, though, he and I were pretty good friends."

"Do you know what school he went to when he moved?" Chloe asked. Rhodes gave her a weird look, perhaps wondering how the question was relevant. Chloe held up her pointer finger, indicating *wait a second*. The wheels were starting to turn now, the gears clicking into place.

"I don't. I'm pretty sure it wasn't far away, though. Somewhere still close by Baltimore."

"How do you know this?"

"I got curious one day a few years back. I did a little Facebook stalking."

"Did you and Richard happen to go to the same school?"

"No. We met at a basketball game when his high school was playing our high school in the state finals."

The wheels continued to turn. Chloe was certain there was something there, but she couldn't quite grasp it yet. She could see by the dawning expression on Rhodes's face that she was starting to get a sense of it, too.

"Ms. Wells, can you recall a time in the past—no matter how insignificant or small—when Bo and Richard might have crossed paths?"

There was silence for a moment as Angie thought about it. When she finally answered, she said: "I can't think of any. Of course, they very well could have met during those high school years and I never knew about it."

There was another question on Chloe's lips but before she could speak it, the door to the office opened. Anderson stepped inside unapologetically, with fire in his eyes. He looked in a hurry, as if he had something urgent to say, but Chloe continued on.

"Do you recall the last time you saw Bo Luntz?"

"Whenever that last day of fifth grade was. So ...Jesus, it's been more than forty years. Funny how well you remember friends from that long ago even when the memories start to fade, huh?"

Before Chloe could answer, Anderson stepped into the room, sliding in right beside Chloe. "Sorry to interrupt, but this is important."

"One second, Detective," Chloe said. "Angie Wells is—"

"There's a third victim," Anderson said, reaching over and ending the call with Angie Wells rather rudely and abruptly. "And this one is recent. So recent, the body is still warm."

Chapter Twelve

When Chloe and Rhodes arrived at the home of Gordon Nettles, there were two policemen standing on the front porch with an absolutely hysterical woman. She was screaming and slapping hard at the shoulders of the brawny officer who was restraining her. Both the occupied brawny officer and his partner regarded Chloe and Rhodes as they came up to the porch. Even though Anderson was accompanying them, bringing up the rear, Chloe and Rhodes went through the motions of showing their IDs. Without a word spoken, they were allowed inside the house.

The body was to the left, past the small foyer, in the dining room. Even before Chloe saw the body itself, she saw the blood. As Anderson had suggested, it was still wet. It might even still be spreading.

"We got the call from the woman out front—the man's wife, Kim. The victim is Gordon Nettles. According to his wife, she came home and found him like that right away."

"No one else was in the house?"

"No."

"How long ago was this?" Rhodes asked.

Anderson checked his phone and did some quick math in his head. "She called nine-one-one thirty-two minutes ago. No more than five minutes had passed between her placing the call and my interrupting your call with Angie Wells."

Chloe entered the dining room and got down close to the body. Right away, she saw that there had been more violence here. Like the other two victims, Nettles had been struck with something heavy on the head. But it looked as if he had been struck four or five times.

Also, just like the others, there was a black sock jammed into his mouth.

Chloe studied the color in the man's face and observed the way the blood was still wet. As gently as she could, she reached out and touched the back of his neck, the one place she knew her own fingerprints would not hinder the work of forensics later on. He was indeed still warm.

"This couldn't have happened any more than two hours ago," she said. "Have you spoken with forensics?"

"Yeah. They're on the way right now."

Chloe wanted to get a look at the sock but did not want to taint any of the evidence. But she also didn't feel like waiting on forensics to arrive. She got to her feet and walked into the adjoined kitchen. As she walked to the sink, she noted that the television was on, showing highlights of a baseball game. She looked under the sink, hoping to find a pair of rubber cleaning gloves. No luck. She then started opening drawers and stopped when she came across one with cooking utensils.

She grabbed a set of silver tongs and then continued opening cabinets and drawers until she found the second item she was looking for: plastic sandwich bags. She grabbed one and returned to the dining room. When she entered, Rhodes saw what she had in her hands and suppressed a rather curious smile.

"Are you serious right now?" Anderson asked.

"I am," she said, handing him the sandwich bag. "This happened very recently. Each second we wait is a wasted one. Hold this bag, would you?"

Knowing what she was about to do, Anderson held the bag, opened up the top, and waited.

Chloe knelt down by the body and used the tongs to grab the crumpled end of the sock. It came out freely and easily, but the feel of it brushing against the victim's teeth was unnerving. When the sock was freed, she gripped the tongs tighter, holding the sock up to the light to get a better look at it.

For some reason, she had been assuming the socks had been of the dressier variety—perhaps the sort you'd wear under a suit or even an office-casual outfit. Instead, the sock she pulled out of Gordon Nettles's mouth was a thick athletic sock. Something about this seemed almost fitting, as if she'd *almost* been expecting it.

"This is the same kind of sock as the other two?" Chloe asked Anderson.

"I'm almost certain, but I can check with forensics."

"This sock being exactly the same as the other two...I think it's safe to assume the killer is bringing the socks with them. The chances of all three victims having the same kind of socks is pretty slim, don't you think?"

"I'd say so," Rhodes said, observing the sock with interest as Chloe slowly dropped it into the bag Anderson still held open.

"At the risk of sounding insensitive, I'd like to try to talk to the wife right now. Again...this murder is so recent...if we can find some sort of trail, I feel like we could catch up to things."

Anderson sighed and looked toward the porch. With none of them talking, it was easy to hear the wife still moaning on the porch. "Which of you is the most compassionate?" he asked.

"That would be Fine," Rhodes said. "Though I think in a case like this, it's best we both be out there."

Without another word said between them, the trio got to their feet and headed back out onto the porch. Chloe had spoken with the spouses of murder victims soon after the murders, but never this soon. She was not looking forward to it. As she slowly approached the officers and the aggrieved wife, Chloe felt her heart breaking a bit.

"Mrs. Nettles?" Chloe said. "I understand this is a terrible time, but I need to ask you some questions. Being that this is so...recent...the faster I can get answers, the sooner we can hopefully find out who did this."

Kim Nettles looked to Chloe and then to Fine, standing behind her. Anderson hung out by the doorway, clearly uneasy with the task at hand. It was clear that Kim was in shock. Her eyes were wild and red from crying. But she also looked dazed and lost, like she had no idea where she was, who she was, or what, exactly, was going on.

Through a wet moan, she said: "Who did this?"

"We don't know, Mrs. Nettles. We were hoping you could help us find out."

"I can...I can try. I just...oh my God, this is real, isn't it? This is really happening?"

Chloe gave a small nod of appreciation to the officers who had been doing their best to console her, dismissing them. The smaller of the two looked incredibly relieved to be freed from the burden. Still, when they walked off of the porch, allowing Chloe and Rhodes to take their place, they did so quietly and with respect.

Chloe reached out and took Kim's hand. She'd read somewhere that the gesture helped to ground the recently bereaved, to keep them physically attached to the world while their brain tried to adjust to the trauma and, in some cases, even started to shut down. Chloe noted that the poor woman's hands were trembling.

"I know it's going to be hard to answer these questions, but it could go a very long way in helping us get answers. But...how old was Gordon?"

"Fifty-three. Same as me..."

"How long were you married?"

"Five years...almost six. I was his second marriage and..."

She trailed off here, shaking her head. She apparently did not want to talk about that. That, or she was quickly losing the spirit to make it through Chloe's questions.

"And do you know if he had been home by himself all day?"

Kim shook her head. A weird croaking sound was coming out of her throat as she did her best to suppress the weeping and moaning they'd heard upon arriving. "No...he usually gets home about an hour before I do. Sometimes more, depending on how slow things are at his work..."

One of those low deep-throated moans escaped her throat and her face seemed to wrinkle up. She let out an anguished sound of pain and sorrow that made Chloe feel incredibly terrible for questioning her in such a state.

She looked over to Rhodes, who was also clearly uncomfortable. She looked away and shook her head.

"Okay, Mrs. Nettles, one last thing and I'll leave you alone. Can you handle one more question?"

Still sobbing, she nodded. Kim surprised Chloe when she leaned into her, as if she might fall over at any moment. Chloe did her best to support her. She also noted, at the same time, that an ambulance and another police car were pulling into the Nettles' driveway.

"Do the names Richard Wells or Bo Luntz mean anything to you?" Chloe asked. "Do you know either of them?"

Kim looked as if she was legitimately trying to think of the names, but Chloe couldn't even imagine trying to think of *anything* other than her dead husband, lying in the floor less than feet away from her.

"No," she said finally. "Not to me. Maybe to Gordon. I don't—"

Her voice cracked here and then she tottered away from Chloe and leaned against the side of the porch. She collapsed against the rail, trying to catch herself. Rhodes acted lightning fast, catching Kim before she could hit the ground. This all occurred while the ambulance parked and two medics came rushing forward.

Kim Nettles continued to sob against Rhodes as the paramedics and the original two officers, along with the new arrivals, came rushing back onto the porch. The sounds of Kim Nettles in an absolute state of emotional agony echoed in Chloe's head, as if letting her know they'd be there to stay until she found the killer.

With that motivation tucked into the back of her head, Chloe walked back inside, her jaw clenched and determination she'd never felt before pushing her along like fire at her heels.

CHAPTER THIRTEEN

Chloe waited until the ambulance had carried Kim Nettles to the hospital before she started looking around her house. She figured she could give the woman at least that much respect. Anderson had followed behind the ambulance, leaving Chloe and Rhodes to search the home while forensics arrived to do their work.

Rhodes walked alongside Chloe as she looked the place over, but she was on the phone. She was talking to someone at FBI headquarters, putting in a rush request on any information they had on Gordon Nettles. Chloe knew it was basic protocol, but based on the very little information they'd had on Bo Luntz and Richard Wells, she wasn't expecting anything to come of it.

Because the television was on—two ESPN commentators currently discussing some new kick-off rule for the upcoming NFL season—Chloe started looking there. The partially worn area along the right side of the couch suggested that either Gordon or Kim preferred this as their seat. She assumed Gordon had been sitting there, watching television, when he got up and was killed.

That means he would have been sitting, she thought. *He had to get up at some point... maybe because he heard the killer come in.*

She looked from the couch, back to the dining room and the patio door. If Gordon had gotten up from the couch and walked into the dining room, that likely meant the killer had come in from the patio door. She also thought about Bo Luntz, dead on his back porch. That gave at least one more connection (one that Richard Wells didn't quite fit): the killer was likely coming in through secondary entrances, skipping the front doors altogether.

She looked around the living room, looking for anything that might tell them more of the story from Nettles's last hour alive but there was nothing. She then went into the kitchen, looking for any signs of a fight or struggle. As she searched, Rhodes ended her call from the bar behind her.

"They'll call back in about fifteen minutes with more information," Rhodes said. "But based off of a cursory glance, it looks like Nettles isn't going to have any red flags."

"I figured as much."

They stepped quietly into the dining room where the forensics guys had been at work for the last ten minutes or so. There were two of them—one dusting for prints and the other taking photos of the body.

"Anything yet?" she asked hopefully.

"Not yet," one of them said. "Give us about half an hour or so. If we find any prints between now and then, we'll let you know."

"We'll be around," Chloe said.

They went back into the living room. Chloe nearly started for the flight of stairs that led to the second floor, planning to check the bedroom. But her gut told her this would be useless. He had been killed downstairs, the killer had likely only ever *been* on this level, so what was the point of looking upstairs?

But then she remembered the photos and phone number she'd found tucked away in the bedroom of Richard Wells. She nearly started up the stairs, but then heard Rhodes from behind her. She was standing in front of a doorway, having just opened the door. She was looking down a set of stairs with some interest on her face.

"Looks and smells like a man cave sort of deal," Rhodes said.

Chloe joined her, asking: "What's a man cave smell like?"

"I'm just assuming. It smells like pizza and feet."

Despite the grisly circumstances, Chloe couldn't help but grin. Leave it to Rhodes to find humor in any given situation.

They started down the stairs together and by the time Chloe was only two steps down, she agreed with Rhodes. It was not a bad smell per se, but one that she felt Kim Nettles may have nagged him about. It smelled like man, plain and simple. Not bad, but not great, either.

When they reached the bottom of the shallow set of stairs, they found themselves in a room that was clearly part of a finished basement. The carpet was plush and the couch that sat in the center of the room was old, scarred, and rather ugly. Still, as man caves went, Chloe didn't think it was that much of a mess.

There was a large flat-screen TV mounted on the wall about five feet away from the couch, complete with a sound bar attached to the bottom. A thin coffee table sat between the television and couch, holding three remotes. The rest of the room was sparsely furnished. There was what looked like a little reading nook over in the corner; a small bookshelf held about fifty titles, mostly works by Stephen King, Lee Child, and Michael Crichton. There were also a few nonfiction books related to outdoor adventure.

The walls were adorned with all sorts of NFL paraphernalia. First and foremost, everything was Washington Redskins–related— a bit uncommon for anyone living in or near Baltimore thanks to the predominance of Ravens fans. There was a signed Chris Cooley jersey, an old program signed by Joe Gibbs, and a framed picture of Nettles at a meet and greet with Clinton Portis (a player Chloe did not know by name and only identified because his name was on a banner behind the pair).

The only things that seemed *not* to be Redskins themed in the entire room were a few pictures that were situated on a small table that sat in one of the far corners. There, an old purple uniform had been mounted in a frame and hung. The jersey boasted the number 36 and the name across the back read: NETTLES.

Chloe went over to the table and looked at the jersey. The color purple flagged something in her memory… something she started to mentally tug at as she looked at the pictures on the table below.

There were only two of them. One showed Nettles playing in what Chloe assumed was a high school football game, running the ball and partially leaping over a defender. The second was a team picture, the players lined up perfectly with the coach right in the center. Everyone was wearing the same purple jersey, the boys dressed in them looking extremely serious—not a single smile among them.

And that's what did it... that's what brought that flagged memory to the front.

She thought of the pictures she had seen on Richard Wells's wall, going up the stairs. Right beside the picture of one of his girls graduating, there had been a picture of a football team. The players in that picture had been wearing purple uniforms.

Chloe was quite certain she was currently looking at the exact same picture, in the man cave of a recently murdered man.

"Rhodes..."

Her partner came over quickly, looking down at the picture. Chloe did not have to waste time wondering if Rhodes had picked up on the connection. This was made pretty obvious when Rhodes said, "Holy shit."

"Nettles and Wells went to high school together," Chloe said. "Played football together, too, I bet."

She picked the picture up and scanned the faces. After about ten seconds, she tapped on the flimsy glass, pointing to a face in the second row.

"Richard Wells," Rhodes said.

"They're the same age, too... give or take a year."

"Okay, but what about Luntz? We know for a fact he didn't go to the same school as Richard Wells. So how does he fit into this?"

"No clue," Chloe said. "I guess that's something we need to find out."

They went back upstairs and, simply for the sake of conducting a thorough search, checked the bedrooms and bathrooms. As Chloe had suspected, they found nothing of use.

By the time they returned downstairs, forensics was wrapping up. At some point in the twenty-two minutes Chloe and Rhodes had been searching the house, the coroner had arrived and had placed the body into a body bag. Chloe wasn't sure if she would ever get used to the almost cavalier way this moment was handled; the body had been bagged and the three men within the room were simply going about their business. She understood it was how the job was done—hell, hers had its own similar situations—but it had always seemed cold and rather distant to her.

The forensics member who had been dusting for prints earlier saw them come in and simply shrugged. "Not a thing. Not a single print on the door, the glass, the floor, the blinds…nothing. There's likely no hair either, though that search will take a bit longer. But being that this is a hardwood floor, if we haven't found anything yet…"

"I know," Chloe said. "Gloves, I assume?"

"Probably. And more than likely a hat or ski mask or something like that, due to the lack of hairs."

"Thanks." She then handed him one of her cards and added: "Please call if anything new comes up."

She and Rhodes ventured back outside, headed for the car. Rhode was already on the phone before they reached the car, speaking to her contact back at the bureau. Chloe listened in as she got behind the wheel.

"We've got a basic confirmation that Richard Wells and Gordon Nettles attended the same high school," she told the research specialist on the other line. "It's very likely they were even in the same graduating class. I need to know as much as I can about both of them, the football team, the school, all of it. And this has to be a priority."

She said nothing else, simply ending the call about five seconds later. She looked ahead as Chloe headed back to the station, a look of determination nearly as strong as the one Chloe had felt earlier coming over her face.

"Looks like we've got a thread," Rhodes said, confident.

"Good. Now let's pull at it until we can unravel the whole damn thing."

CHAPTER FOURTEEN

Chloe and Rhodes had barely had time to sit back down in front of Rhodes's notes on the whiteboard before they received their call back from the bureau. Rhodes answered it, set it to speaker mode, and took her place by the whiteboard. Chloe stood leaning against the table, listening as the details came in, leading them closer to ending this case.

"You called it," a woman's voice said from the bureau end of the phone. "Richard Wells and Gordon Nettles were both in the same graduating class and attended Summit Hills High School. The football team was the Cougars."

"Could you confirm that either of them played football?" Chloe asked.

"Not yet. I placed a call to the school to get the information, but, being that it's after five o'clock, I was directed to a voicemail service."

"That's not a big deal," Rhodes said. "We can speak to one of the wives to get verification on that. If we asked around the precinct here, I wonder if we might even get lucky enough to find someone else who went to school with them—maybe get a yearbook or something."

"Anything else you need from me?" the woman asked.

"No thanks," Rhodes said. "This is more than enough."

Chloe killed the call while Rhodes wrote down *Summit Mills High School*, connecting it to Wells and Nettles on the board.

"Well, I'm not about to bother Kim Nettles," Chloe said, pulling out her own phone. "Maybe Sherry Luntz can answer the football question for us."

"Maybe even Angie Wells." Rhodes pointed, scribbling Angie's name on the board and connecting it to Bo Luntz. "Remember, they were childhood friends."

"Which, even if there was no football involved in Luntz's case, connects all three of the victims in a roundabout way."

Chloe felt a stirring of excitement as she placed the call to Sherry Luntz. She knew they weren't quite on the precipice of the huge break that would seal the case, but she could feel them starting to corner it.

Sherry Luntz's phone rang three times before she answered it. "Hello?"

"Mrs. Luntz, this is Agent Chloe Fine. Please know that I would not call you with further questions unless it was very important. But there has been a third victim and we believe we may have found a link to all three victims."

"A...a third? Oh my God..."

"Are you okay? Could you answer just one or two questions?"

"Of course...anything I can do to help."

"Did your husband play football in high school?"

"He...hold on, what? That's a strange question." She chuckled, as if she had legitimately been surprised by the question. But even in her chuckle, Chloe could hear her pain and loss.

"I know. I apologize, but it may be very relevant."

"He did play in high school. The Summit Hills Cougars. He likes to tell stories about it and I tell him it makes him sound like Al Bundy from that show *Married With Children*. But one of the years he was playing, back in the late eighties or early nineties, I don't remember which...they won the state championship."

Chloe realized that Sherry was still referring to him in the present tense...as if he was still alive.

"But now, you said that the two of you attended different high schools, right?"

"That's right.

"Would you happen to know if he always attended the same high school?"

"You know … I don't think so. His family moved like four times between the time he started middle school to around his ninth or tenth grade year. Not sure why. It seemed foolish, I guess, because they always stayed around this area. But no … I don't think he spent all four years of his high school years at the same school."

Chloe felt a stirring of excitement in her guts at this. That one comment meant that maybe there *was* a school connection between the victims.

"Mrs. Luntz, do you happen to know the name Gordon Nettles?"

There was a slight hesitation on her end before she answered. "No, I don't think so. Honestly … it *sounds* familiar, but it's not anyone I know."

"Someone Bo knew, perhaps?"

"Maybe. I'm sorry … I just don't know for sure."

"That's okay. You've been a tremendous help and I hope this helps us get you some answers."

After thanking Sherry Luntz for her time, Chloe ended the call and looked at the board. She looked at Rhodes's scribbling for a while longer and started to pace the room. "If Luntz moved that many times in a short period of time, there *is* a good chance he ended up at the same high school as Wells and Nettles."

Rhodes grinned and grabbed her phone up from the table. "There's a very easy way to figure this out, you know? And quite honestly, I feel like an idiot for not thinking of it until now."

Chloe almost asked what her idea was but then saw that she was opening up her Facebook app. When the app was opened, she went to the search bar and typed in Bo Luntz's name. She scrolled through the several selections until she found the right one. When his profile was pulled up, she scrolled a bit more as Chloe watched over her shoulder.

Sure enough, right there in his bio, his high school and college were listed.

He had Summit Hills listed as his graduating high school.

"And there's a link to all three victims," Chloe said, resisting the urge to give a little fist pump in the air.

"So why are they being killed?" Rhodes said. "And why the black sock?"

"That's hanging me up, too. The pictures we saw of the Cougars team all had the players wearing white socks."

"Are we safe to assume that it's even high school related?" Rhodes asked.

"I'd think so. There has to be more than twenty high schools in the Baltimore area. Probably more. The fact that all three victims not only attended the same one but also all played on a championship football team together..."

"Yeah, I see that," Rhodes said. "But Jesus...forty-some years later. Who holds a grudge for that long?"

"Maybe someone from a rival football team?" Chloe suggested.

"I'd say I don't think people take football that seriously...but we just came out of the Redskins shrine downstairs."

"And apparently, the Cougars players held on to those high school memories. Both Wells and Nettles thought enough of their football days in high school to frame those team photos."

"I'd like to talk to Angie Wells again," Rhodes said.

Chloe nodded in agreement but then checked the time on her phone. It was 9:45 at night and she remembered Angie stating that she had a plane to catch out to Baltimore for her ex-husband's funeral.

"As much as I hate to say it, I think we should wait. The poor woman—who already seems to not really care much that her husband has died, mind you—just got off of a plane to bury the man she married. I think it can wait until tomorrow."

Rhodes sat down, agreeing without saying anything. Chloe noted the look on her face, though. It was one of severe disappointment. It was the same feeling Chloe was wrestling with. She knew that striking while the iron was hot was their best bet. With Nettles having been killed and discovered all within less than an hour and a half, that would have been the perfect time to roll with leads and discoveries. But Chloe knew that they had missed their window. Sure, they still had this new exciting connection with football, but for now, the sting of excitement was starting to fade.

It was this realization that made her realize there was no way she was going to sleep. They had this confirmed connection. More than that, they knew that a very good source of information was now in town and not hiding away in Rhode Island. Yes…she had made the suggestion to leave Angie Wells be until the morning, but now she felt that it would be irresponsible to let it go until morning. This killer was striking quickly. There was no time at all to waste.

"You know," Chloe said, "I think we should go ahead and call her. It couldn't hurt, right?"

"I think you were right," Rhodes said. "I think it might be in bad taste this late, the day before Richard's funeral."

"We need to do something. We can't just let this sit…not with the new lead."

"It'll be okay. Let's just get some sleep."

Chloe considered it but then shook her head. "No. Even if Angie Wells refuses to speak with me, there has to be something else …"

"Fine…I say this with respect and maybe even love. You need to rest. You've been on this like a madwoman. I've seen the look on your face through this. You're clearly sidetracked and, at the same time, motivated by what's going on with your sister. You can't wear yourself ragged with *both* these cases. You need to sleep."

It wasn't until Rhodes mentioned Danielle that Chloe realized she hadn't even thought about her sister for the better part of three hours. And because Rhodes's comment had made her realize this, the spark of shame and anger that rose up in her reared its head at her partner. It was a flash of quick anger that came out of nowhere but took over rather quickly.

"Sidetracked?"

"You know what I mean," Rhodes said, her expression indicating she knew she had perhaps crossed a line. But, as tough as ever, she wasn't about to take it back.

"Tell you what," Chloe said with venom in her tone. "Why don't you go ahead and get some sleep? This killer is averaging a person every two days. They're up to three and no one has even sniffed after them, so God only knows what they think they're capable of.

And we have no way of knowing how many victims are on their list. So, you go ahead and sleep. But I'm going to find *some* way to keep moving on."

"Chloe, I—"

With no idea of where she would go or how she would get there, Chloe exited the room. She did so as calmly as she could, pushed by that anger. Yet, as she neared the doors, she realized that the anger she felt toward Rhodes was quickly deescalating into shame. Shame over not being as concerned about her sister as she felt she should be. Shame over being so close to a lead and then feeling it slowly slip away as night swept over the world.

She stepped out into the night and walked to the bureau car she and Rhodes had taken out. She sat in it, pretty sure she knew Rhodes well enough to know her partner would sit in front of that whiteboard, trying to put more pieces together until she had a eureka moment or until her eyes slipped closed. Still, as upset as she was at her partner, Chloe could not just leave her here at the station without a car.

Looking out into the night and now unable to take her mind off of her sister, she called Detective Anderson's cell phone. She hated to call him at such a late hour but was beyond stopping herself with such courtesies.

Surprisingly, when he answered on the second ring, he did not sound all that upset. She could hear the TV going in the background as he said: "Hello?"

"Anderson … this is Agent Fine. Rhodes and I are going to split up for a bit. Who do I need to call to borrow one of the precinct cars?"

Anderson chuckled and then gave her the name and number of the facilities manager. She then placed that call and once again was surprised that no one seemed to mind that she was calling at such a late hour. Less than fifteen minutes after making the call to Anderson, Chloe was behind the wheel of one of the Central District's common sedans.

She still had one more call to make and she did not think the person on the other end was going to be as easygoing as Anderson and the facilities manager. She called anyway because she felt she had to: for the three victims, for her sister, for herself. She had to keep moving, had to keep her mind and this case pushed forward constantly.

She called Angie Wells, a knot forming in her stomach as the phone rang in her ear. When she heard the click of someone answering on the other line, the little digital clock on the car's dashboard read 10:16.

"Hello?"

Angie's voice was irritated. The single word had enough inflection in it to clue the caller in to the fact that she did not appreciate receiving calls from people she did not know this late.

"Ms. Wells, it's Agent Fine. I spoke with you briefly when you spoke with my partner earlier today."

"Yes, I remember."

"I am terribly sorry to bother you at such an hour but we have a new lead and I hope you can help solidify it and perhaps even lead us closer to more answers. Would you be willing to give me just five minutes?"

She could hear Angie sighing on the other end. The silence that followed was a heavy one. "I'll do you one better," she finally said. "I'm staying at the Hilton Garden Inn—the Inner Harbor one. Meet me out here in half an hour to buy me a drink and I'll give you all the time you'd like."

Chloe didn't even have to think about it. Her luck with late-night calls had been exceptional tonight and she wasn't about to look that particular gift horse in the mouth. "I'll see you at the bar in half an hour."

With that, she cranked the car and drove into the city. She did her best to keep Danielle away from the center of her mind but it was impossible. Her sister may as well have been sitting in the passenger seat with her, griping about her speed, her rudeness in calling people so late, and her inability to truly escape her past once and for all.

Chapter Fifteen

Angie Wells's drink of choice was rum and Coke and from the looks of it, the one Chloe purchased her shortly after they sat down at the bar had not been her first one of the night—not by a long shot. She was a waifish woman who carried her age well but her alcohol, not so much. Still, she was a pleasant drunk. So what if she slurred her words a bit and leaned in too close, ignoring any general rules about personal space. She wasn't drunk just yet but it was clear that she intended to be that way before the night was over.

"You say you have a new lead now?" Angie asked, getting right to the point.

"We do. And if you can help iron it out, it would help in a tremendous way."

"I'll do what I can."

"We discovered today that all three of the victims played football in high school. And all three of them played for—"

"The Summit Hills Cougars, right?"

"That's right," Chloe said. "There were quite a few of the players we're looking into that had gone to previous schools before coming to Summit Hill, and it muddied the waters a bit. Made it harder for us to make the connection."

Angie sipped from her drink and shook her head at the same time. She set the glass down and had a faraway look in her eyes. "If I had a dollar for every time Richard told me a story about that championship year ... well, I probably would have never left him because I'd be rich and wouldn't have cared that he neglected me."

"Did you also go to Summit Hills?"

"Oh yeah. I was a cheerleader for the Cougars. I say that with a bit of shame. God, I was stupid back then."

"Did you and Richard date in high school?"

"Sort of. We were into each other and messed around a bit. It was pretty heavy. Somewhere between love and lust, you know? But it didn't last. We didn't get back together and get married until much later. One of those random meetings years after high school, you know. It was at the grocery store of all places."

"Was the relationship in high school a very serious one?"

"No. It was mostly just dirty talk and flirting innocently. He was the running back for the Cougars. Man, he ..."

She stopped here, looking down at her drink and then up at Chloe as if she had said something particularly stupid. "Wait. Just a while ago, you said *all three* victims played football. But when you spoke to me this morning, there had only been two victims: Richard and then Bo Luntz."

Chloe nodded and wished she had a drink. She thought about it for a while but wasn't going to be that irresponsible—especially not while driving a loaner from the Baltimore police. "You're right. There was a third victim discovered just this afternoon. And if you were a cheerleader for the Cougars that championship year, I'm going to guess you know him. Gordon Nettles."

"Jesus," Angie said, and took another sip of her drink. "Yeah, I knew him. We um ... well, never dated per se, but we did ... things. Let's just leave it at that."

"Can you confirm that he was also on the team?" Chloe asked.

"Yeah. Gordon was the wide receiver. A damned good one, too. Usually, the quarterback is the star of the show, but Gordon was the star player on the Cougars that year."

"If you knew all three of them, even just a little bit, you must know if they were friends, right? Were they like a group?"

"I think Bo and Gordon were somewhat close that year, but not because they were friends. It was the fact that they were on the team, you know? I can't be sure. Richard was friends with Gordon for sure, though. They had something of a reputation for drinking and sleeping their way around the school."

"Is there anything else you remember about them? Or maybe even just the team itself?"

"I know they all hated those purple uniforms," she said with a smile. "Even after we were married and high school was ten years behind us, Richard complained about it."

"Anything juicier than that?"

Angie nodded and downed the rest of her glass. She then slid it to the bartender's side of the bar and looked at Chloe. Chloe took it as an unspoken request and nodded. *Yes, you can have another drink if you keep talking.*

"It sucks to think of your ex-husband—a *dead* ex-husband now—in such a way, but yes, there is plenty I remember. There were several of the players on that championship team that were just flat out bullies. On the surface, I think most of the students and faculty just thought they did it out of showing a tough façade … that it was harmless, you know? Boys will be boys and all of that bullshit."

She stopped here as the bartender collected the empty glass and set to making a second one. Chloe took the time to note that the bar was fairly empty with the exception of a table of twenty-somethings on the other side of the bar.

"What kind of bullies?" Chloe asked.

"They were just mean. I can tell you, though, that Richard regretted it all. He sort of turned himself around after we had our first daughter."

"Can you remember anyone specifically they might have been mean to?"

"Mostly to the second-string players, but like I said … I don't think it was anything terrible. Just macho nonsense. But you know …"

Angie seemed to go blank here, staring down at her drink as if she had totally forgotten what she was talking about. She then looked up at Chloe after about five seconds. A look of understanding floated in her eyes; it looked almost haunting in the dim lights of the bar.

"Ms. Wells?"

"It's…well, I forgot about it, I think. Maybe intentionally. But there was one person that a lot of the guys on the team used to…I don't know…used to torment."

"Do you remember who it was?"

"Yes," she said. Her eyes still looked far away as she dredged the memories up. From the look on her face, she did not want to see these memories at all. "I heard them calling him names a few times…maybe even pushing him around at practices. But there were rumors…"

"What was the name?" Chloe asked.

"Matt Sawyer. He was the water boy for the team, and sometimes the coach's errand boy. Thin rail of a kid…cute, though. I think he was a freshman the year they won the championship. Some of the players would act like they were his friends and then embarrass him when there was a crowd around. That sort of thing."

"Did you ever actually *see* any of the players mistreating him?"

"Yeah. Again, though, in high school, you think nothing of it. Little shoves in the hallway, wedgies here and there. God, I…I saw it all back then and never said anything." She downed some more of her second drink and when she set it down, dropped a line that would stick with Chloe for a very long time. "We were all just a bunch of little monsters back in high school, weren't we? Good student, bad student, it didn't matter…"

"Would you happen to know if he's still local to this area?"

"According to his Facebook profile, he is. But I haven't even checked in years. Last I saw online, he does something in real estate here in the city."

Chloe felt herself wanting to leave right there and then, again looking past the fact that it had gotten quite late. Even if she could locate a location or number for a real estate worker by the name of Matt Sawyer, any meeting with him would have to wait until the following day.

Still, she had everything she needed out of Angie Wells. She slapped a twenty down on the bar and got to her feet. "Ms. Wells, this has been a huge help. I'm very sorry for your recent loss and hope you make it through tomorrow okay."

"Thanks. I think I'll be fine. Both of my girls are here with me and ... yeah ..."

Again, she seemed to zone out. Chloe walked away rather awkwardly, leaving the bar area and entering the lobby. As she walked to the doors, she hesitated for a moment and then walked to the front desk. One of the two people at the desk greeted her with a smile and a "How are you tonight?"

"I'm good. I know it might seem old school, but would you happen to have a phone book back there?"

The woman—on the younger side, maybe thirty at most—smiled and reached under the counter. Chloe heard a drawer opening and then the woman handed her a large yellow phone book for the Baltimore area. Chloe opened it and thumbed to the back, looking for local real estate agent listings. She felt like she was excavating some ancient creature as she went through the pages, finding a new appreciation for the agents who had come before her—without the aid of internet and smartphones.

In the back of the book, about halfway through the real estate agent listings, she saw the name she had just heard from Angie Wells. Apparently, Matt Sawyer was indeed still in the Baltimore area. His number and office location were listed in a large font. Chloe used her phone to snap a picture of the ad before sliding the phone book back across the counter.

She headed back out into the night, feeling that tomorrow would be pivotal to the case. With this Matt Sawyer lead, she dared to hope tomorrow might even bring them to the killer.

CHAPTER SIXTEEN

Chloe knew she'd made too much of a scene to simply call up Rhodes to see where she had gotten a room. Besides that, Chloe honestly didn't feel like being around anyone. So, following her meeting with Angie Wells, Chloe headed back to the Central District station. She got there at 11:46 and though she could feel sleep making its daily suggestion, she knew she wouldn't be able to rest … not for a while, anyway.

The precinct was virtually empty. As she walked down the corridor to the office she and Rhodes had been using, she passed by four officers and one woman who looked a little out of place—likely the late-night secretary or a dispatch assistant.

She checked in to the office, just in case Rhodes had stayed in late, but the room was empty. Chloe looked at the whiteboard, feeling a bit of regret for the way she had behaved. After all, Rhodes had absolutely nothing to do with her personal drama. And no matter how Chloe wanted to paint it, it was the mess with Danielle and her father that had caused her to get testy; it had not been anything Rhodes had done.

Chloe left the room behind and found Anderson's workstation. He had given her and Rhodes permission to use anything of his earlier in the day, and this was the first time either of them had taken him up on it. She punched in her guest credentials and logged into the precinct's system. She then typed in the name *Matt Sawyer* and got to work.

It took less than thirty seconds for her to determine that the Matt Sawyer that Angie Wells had mentioned did not have a criminal record. She even had a quick look in the simplified driving database and saw that Matt Sawyer was squeaky clean there as well.

Her next step was to go online to see what she could find. First and foremost, his name was fairly prevalent in terms of Realtors in the Baltimore area. He'd won several awards in the past six years and tended to work with real estate trends listed in to the mid to high six figures. It was here, in one of the articles she found, that she saw Matt Sawyer for the first time.

His smile seemed genuine, the look of a man that loves his job. In the picture, he was standing by a SOLD sign in the front yard of a gorgeous house. Sawyer looked to be rather small statured. It was hard to tell through the dress slacks and button-down shirt he was wearing, but he also looked quite thin.

The coroner suspected the killer might be short, Chloe reminded herself.

It was a weak lead, but she was willing to take whatever she could get. She typed in Matt Sawyer's office number and address into her Notes app and then shut down Anderson's workspace. She sat there for a moment, wondering how she should close out the night. Her phone told her that it was 12:25 a.m. She didn't want to call Rhodes and risk waking her; she figured she could find her own room somewhere in the city and they could reconnect then.

But as she got to her feet, she realized just how tired she was. The idea of getting behind the wheel again, checking into a room, and then getting settled down was just too much. She walked back to the office with the whiteboard and considered just pushing a chair against the wall and crashing.

But then another idea occurred to her—an idea based on something one of her instructors had discussed back at the academy. It had sounded like a rock star idea at the time but now, faced with actually doing it, Chloe wasn't too sure.

She walked down the remainder of the hallway and turned to the right. A door at the end of this hall led her directly to the holding cells. There were currently three that were occupied, but four others that were empty. She made her way to the end of the dimly lit, cold-colored room, and took the cell all the way at the end so that none of the other occupants of the other cells would be within sight. Being that it was unoccupied, the door was opened just a bit. She went into the cell and lay down on the cot. The sheets smelled of bleach and the pillow felt like cardboard. Still, she was barely afforded enough time to wonder about the odd nature of what she was doing and just how morbid her sleeping choice was, before sleep reached up and snatched her.

It pulled her down quickly and, much to Chloe's chagrin, it had nothing but horror waiting for her.

The dream was dizzying and similar to what some might refer to as lucid dreaming, at first. Chloe was flying over what appeared to be an endless expanse of woodland. Below, something was tearing through the forests. The flying version of herself swooped down, passing through treetops and branches to get a better look. The closer she got, the more she learned about the shape that was rushing through the forest. It was small. It was fast. And it was very scared.

As she descended lower, plummeting now like someone falling from a building, she saw that this moving shape was Danielle. She was dressed in a white T-shirt and jeans. The shirt was caked in blood and dirt, as was her hair. She was running impossibly fast, panting from the exertion, and looking back over her shoulder as she ran forward.

Chloe paused and looked back, her soaring coming to a stop. Another object was moving through the forest—equally as fast but much more menacing. Within seconds, she saw this object too. It was her father—Aiden Fine, chasing after Danielle.

Chloe started flying again, bursting through the forests in a shapeless and detached sort of way. She wasn't sure how she could help Danielle but she had to try; she had to at least catch up with her sister to see if there was anything she could do. As she neared

Danielle, she watched as her sister suddenly veered hard to the left and hunkered down onto the ground. She crawled to an enormous tree and slid herself into its hollow, a dark oval shape nestled between the roots.

Danielle watched as her father came rushing forward. He went directly to the tree in which she was hiding. Chloe saw in that moment that he held a knife, the gleam of its blade muted by a bloodstain.

As Aiden reached the tree and started to come around it, Chloe's position from above changed. There was a flash of darkness, followed by the sensation of falling. And then, just as her father came to the hollow of the trees, Chloe realized what had happened.

It was *her* within the hollow now. It was *her* being chased by her father.

With this realization, Aiden Fine drew back his knife. There was a maniacal smile on his face, as if he were enjoying every single moment of this.

The knife came surging forward, passing through roots and bark as if they were nothing more than gelatin. Chloe screamed as her father leered in at her, the knife swinging toward her chest…

Chloe awoke, feeling a scream in her throat. She swallowed it down as she shot up in terror, her hands instantly going to her chest, where her father had been aiming the knife.

She looked around, startled. At first, she had no idea where she was or how she had gotten there. But the feel of the starchy sheets beneath her and the odd glare of dim overhead lights on the tile floor slowly clued her in.

Her disorientation faded slowly as she swung her feet out of bed. She had a terrible after-nap taste in her mouth, which made her realize that her bags were still in the back of the sedan that Rhodes had taken to the hotel.

"You, you okay down there?" a man's voice asked.

Chloe turned her head in the direction of the other holding cells. Apparently, her little dream had made her vocal.

"Yes," she croaked, still not fully awake.

"You was fussing and hollering real bad," the man said.

Chloe said nothing to this. She grabbed her phone from the side of the bed and saw that it was 6:05. She stretched a bit and then left the cell. When she passed by the others in holding, she avoided eye contact, not wanting to even imagine what sort of sounds the dream had pushed out of her lungs.

She made it three steps down the hall before she saw Detective Anderson. He was coming out of the office she and Rhodes had been using. He looked at her, a little confused, and waited for her by the door.

"Getting an early start?" he asked.

"Sort of. I worked too late … didn't bother going to get a motel. So I just crashed in one of the holding cells. I hope that was okay."

"Fine with me," he said. "But just between you and I, those mattresses suck."

"Oh, yes, I know. Hey … weird question. I don't suppose you have toothbrushes around here anywhere, do you?"

He grinned, unable to help himself. "We do, actually. We keep some on reserve for the prisoners in the holding cells. Hold on one second and I can grab you one."

"Thanks."

He continued to grin at her, almost as if he wanted to say something else. After about two seconds, he decided not to. He turned away and headed toward the front of the building. As Chloe watched him go, her thoughts turned almost randomly to Danielle.

Seeing her in the dream, running through the forest from their father … that image pained her more than the imagery of her father thrusting a knife toward her.

She's okay, some wiser part of her said. *She's quick-witted, stubborn, and a real bad-ass, whether you want to admit it or not.*

The feeling that came over her then wasn't quite relief, but almost a strange sort of calm. She felt deep in her heart that this was the case—that Danielle could take care of herself and was likely okay. She was almost certain of this. She wondered if it came down to some weird twin thing, an almost supernatural connection between them.

Don't be stupid, that same part of her spoke up. *It's hope. And whether you believe it or not, hope is sometimes a fine thing to have.*

As she stood there, waiting for Anderson to bring her a tooth-brush and toothpaste, she tried to let this sink in, to let her mid focus on that. It worked for the most part, but she was still unable to shake the dream of a blood-splattered Danielle running through the forest with their crazy and deeply troubled father on her heels.

CHAPTER SEVENTEEN

Danielle's watch read 2:37. She was exhausted, as she had been unable to sleep. It was the one part of her plan she had not really chiseled out, Honestly, she had not expected it to take this long to get a confession out of him. She figured they'd stay here for maybe a few hours. She'd then unbind him and leave him out here while she drove back to DC.

She wasn't going to kid herself about killing him anymore. She simply didn't have it in her. She thought such a realization would be devastating, but it actually cheered her a bit. Apparently, she wasn't as evil and vile as she had assumed.

But he was not making any kind of confessions. She'd hoped that as he got worn down, the confession would come easier. He hadn't slept, either. With his arms pulled up over his head the way they were, it basically made it impossible. She'd watched him drift off a single time, but when he'd leaned forward a bit as he dozed, the ropes had kept his arms tight, pinning his shoulders back at a painful angle.

That had been about an hour ago. Ever since he had been yanked awake by the pain and his awkward posture, they had been staring at one another in the darkness. Slight and muted shafts of moonlight spilled in through a small hole in the ceiling and what had once been a window by the far wall. It was enough for her to see his face, the worn out expression and legitimate fear that had washed over him.

In planning this whole thing, she thought seeing him afraid would make her feel in charge—that it would give her a sense of power. But so far, all it did was make her feel like she was manipulating her father. Some small and stubborn part of her seemed to still be a nine-year-old girl, shouting: *This is what you get for not loving me. This is what you get for taking my mother away from me and leaving me loveless and feeling unwanted.*

She supposed, deep down, that she had turned out to be just as sadistic as he was. It was why she found it almost natural to think that she would just have to kill him if she did not get the confession out of him. And one of those things was going to have to happen soon. Danielle knew that she was getting tired—perhaps *too* tired. If she stayed awake much longer and nothing happened, she could get sloppy. Worse than that, her emotions would get the better of her; she knew this all too well.

She went to her pack, stretching her legs and feeling a slight pins-and-needles tingle in her backside from sitting on the pallet stack most of the day. As she stood, she turned on the digital recorder, wanting it ready in case he slipped up.

As she rummaged through her bag, she saw the pack of cigarettes and nearly pulled them out to head outside to smoke. But she fought the urge and went to the bottom of the bag where the gun was waiting.

She'd chosen a gun because the idea of sinking a knife into him made her queasy. Apparently, her desire for justice and revenge was not strong enough to overcome her revulsion to blood and all other gruesome things. She figured a gun would be faster and, according to what she had read on Google, would not cause all that much bloodshed if the bullet was placed directly between the eyes and at an angle.

She removed the gun—a compact Springfield 1911 she had picked up a few years back after a particularly nasty break-up—and carried it toward her father. She did it casually, as if she might be offering him a sandwich rather than a bullet to the forehead. He saw what she held and recoiled sleepily. But he said nothing. Neither of them had spoken a word for the better part of four hours. They were out of words, empty of things to say. Besides, Danielle had told him if he opened his mouth for anything other than water or to give a confession of the misery he had put her mother through, she would kill him.

"Ready to confess yet?" Danielle asked.

He let out a few muffled noises from behind the gag. She'd given him ample chances to speak by taking it off but he had refused to say anything now. He shook his head, his eyes trained on the pistol. With her free hand, Danielle tore the gag away. It slipped down and hung around his neck.

He then did something Danielle had not expected. He let out a scream—a cry for help. It was so unexpected, Danielle jumped back, fumbling with the gun. Aiden did not say any words, just a simple scream for help, hoping someone would hear him.

Caught by surprise, Danielle reacted on sheer impulse. She drew back the hand holding the pistol and punched him in the face. There was a dry clicking noise as the gun slammed into his mouth. She felt his teeth in that *clink* and could actually feel it when his bottom lip split open.

She jerked her hand away quickly—not just to prevent herself from being sprayed with blood from his lip, but because she had been so surprised by her own actions. But at the same time, she realized that even that small action of surprise and disgust could easily make her appear to be the weak one here.

Gritting her teeth and battling with a growing tide of emotion that seemed to be pushing out from her heart, Danielle stepped forward and placed the gun in his face. She saw that his lip was indeed split open, blood slowly trickling down it and off his chin.

Oh my God, I'm going to do it, she thought. *I'm really going to kill him. Right now. No more delaying or wishing. Just pull the trigger and...*

But she couldn't do it. That tide of emotion was growing larger—so large, in fact, that she feared it would sweep her away at any moment. The gun, though small and purchased specifically for her small hands, felt as heavy as a boulder in her hands. Her arms trembled and something inside of her felt like it was about to explode. Maybe her heart...maybe her soul.

She stepped forward, placing the gun to his forehead. This close, she would probably get some blood on her. She didn't care. She had to...

She let out a cry of frustration, that rising tide inside of her now overwhelming everything.

She stepped away and lowered the gun.

"Danielle…"

She wheeled back on him and leered into his face. The blood from his busted lip was covering most of his chin now. That, plus the look of sheer uncertainty in his eyes made him look like a frightened child rather than a wounded older man.

"Not a word…"

She wanted to shoot him. God, she wanted him dead so badly. Just looking at him, bleeding and afraid and trying to play the victim…it was too much. She reached out and slid the gag back up over his mouth, wiping blood away as she did so. He didn't even bother trying to fight against it this time.

Danielle went back to her bag and pulled out the cigarettes. She hurried outside, where the darkness of night felt thick and humid. She pressed herself against the side of the old building and felt like she could very well be the only person on earth. Her hands trembled as she worked the lighter to the cigarette she had placed in her mouth.

What the hell are you going to do now? You can't kill him, you don't have it in you. After all the time and fantasies you've put into thinking about this moment… and you're too scared to do it.

She hated to admit it, but it was all true. And she had no idea what to do now.

There, hidden by the night and the looming shape of the old slaughterhouse, Danielle started to weep. She sank down against the wall, sliding until her butt hit the dirt She shook and cried, the cigarette falling out of her mouth.

She had to fix this. Well…there was no way *she* could fix it. She'd need help.

She'd have to find a phone tomorrow and call Chloe. Chloe would know what to do. Even if it was too late to save herself and there were consequences staring at her down the road, she had to make the call.

That is, of course, if Chloe would even take her call at all.

CHAPTER EIGHTEEN

Chloe parked in front of Matt Sawyer's house at 7:10 a.m., just a few hours after springing awake from a nightmare in the holding cell. The house was beautiful, located in one of the premier housing developments just on the outskirts of the city. Before she opened her car door to go knock on the Sawyers' door and start their day off miserably, Chloe thought about calling Rhodes. It would be the professional thing to do—the courteous thing to do at the very least.

But what then? Sit here and wait for Rhodes to show up? It wasn't like they needed to be attached at the hip. Knowing that it likely wasn't the right thing to do, Chloe went ahead and stepped out of the car. She made her way up the elegantly cared for sidewalk, glazed to look almost slick. As she made her way up onto the porch and prepared to knock, she could hear the voices of children from inside. She cringed, really not looking forward to questioning a man about murders in front of his children, guilty or not.

But she'd been in this situation before and felt confident she could handle it well. She steeled up her courage and knocked on the door. Right away she heard little footsteps rushing toward the door. This was followed by a man's hushed voice, telling the owner of those footsteps that they better not answer that door.

After a few more seconds and some shuffling noises behind the closed door, it was finally answered. Chloe found herself looking at Matt Sawyer. There was a smile on his face, fading as he regained composure of whatever had just occurred with his kids behind the door. He gave Chloe a curious look but remained pleasant, despite the early hour.

"Can I help you?" he asked. "I'm sure you know it's a bit early."

"I do know that," Chloe said. She spied over his shoulder and saw a girl of about eight hopping down the hallway on one leg, trying to put a shoe on. She wore a very pretty dress and had her hair up in pigtails. "And I am very sorry to bother you, as it seems you have kiddos you're trying to get ready for church."

"Well, my wife, God bless her, handles that on Sunday mornings. When I try to dress them, it's just one big mess. Anyway ... I ask again ... can I help you?"

Chloe spoke as softly as she could, leaning in a bit. She showed her ID as she said, "I'm Agent Chloe Fine, with the FBI. I was hoping to have a word with you."

He looked shocked, but not quite scared. He glanced quickly back into his house. Chloe could hear a woman—she assumed Sawyer's wife—speaking sternly to one of the kids.

"Can I ask what it's about?"

"I'm investigating three murders within the area. Your name came up in the string of information I'm following."

He nodded, almost as if he'd been expecting it. "Three now?"

"Did you already know about two?"

"I did," he said. "Facebook high school graduation pages. The two I knew about were Richard Wells and Bo Luntz."

"And you went to high school with them, correct?"

"Oh yeah," Sawyer said, almost regretfully.

"Mr. Sawyer, I'd really appreciate it if you could come down to the station to be questioned. We're having issues finding real links between the deceased and—"

"Who was the third, if you don't mind me asking?"

Chloe hesitated. If Matt Sawyer was indeed the killer, he was playing the part of clueless suspect incredibly well. "No, I'm afraid I can't tell you that," she finally answered. "Not here, not yet."

"Can you give me a moment to discuss this with my wife?"

"Sure. I'll be right here, waiting."

He nodded and closed the door. She tried to figure out how she felt about Sawyer. Usually, her gut came up with a decision about a potential suspect right away: either guilty or likely innocent. But with Matt Sawyer, her gut seemed unable to decide. He was playing the nice guy thing a little too well, as if he was putting up a front.

But she had also learned not to assume the worst about people. It was one of the key things she was still trying to teach herself. Given the sort of crimes she had seen—not to mention the drama with her father that had followed her through most of her life—it was a hard thing to do.

Three minutes later, Matt Sawyer came back out onto the porch. His wife followed behind him, looking over his shoulder.

"Should I be worried?" she asked Chloe.

"I don't think so," Chloe answered, mainly because it was the first thing that came to her mind.

The wife then looked to her husband and said: "Let me know if you need to be picked up or anything."

"I will."

They then shared a kiss and Matt Sawyer closed the door. With a shrug and a look of utter dismay, he looked down at Chloe's car. "I assume you're driving...so lead the way."

While Matt Sawyer did not seem all that surprised that Chloe wanted to question him, he seemed equally unsurprised when he heard the name of the third victim. Once Chloe gave him the name, he simply nodded and sipped slowly from the cup of coffee she had brought him from the precinct break room.

"You don't look surprised," she said.

"I don't think I am...not really."

"Mr. Sawyer, do you have any idea why your name might have come up?"

"Sure. It's because if there was ever anyone to cross the paths of those three men that would get some satisfaction out of seeing them dead, it would be me."

"And why is that?"

"Because they tormented me in high school. I assume someone close to them told you as much."

"Yes, they did. Would you care to elaborate on the word *torment?*"

For the first time, Matt Sawyer look to be a bit out of sorts. He looked away from Chloe, his eyes going toward the ceiling. Chloe sipped from her own cup of coffee as she waited for him to respond.

"Will this go on the record?" he asked.

"If it leads to an arrest or helps break the case, it might."

"And you have no leads as of right now?"

"I'm being honest, Mr. Sawyer, you're it. Based on what I know, you're the only person we've come across who would have the motive to kill Bo Luntz and Richard Wells. The jury is still out on Gordon Nettles."

"Well, he'd be on the list, too."

"And why is that?"

He sighed and sat rigidly back in his chair. "I suppose because I wasn't as athletic or as cool as them. I was the water boy for the football team they all played on. I helped accumulate statistics and things of that nature as well. From time to time, I had to go into the locker room. And because I wasn't one of the players and because I wore glasses, I was fair game."

"Fair game for what?"

"Name calling and … It was forty years ago, so it was abuse that would likely get a kid kicked out of school these days. But back then … nope. Just rough boys being boys. Plus, they were on the football team, so …"

"What sort of abuse are we talking about?"

"It was never fighting. No punches or kicks or anything like that—though that might have been better. No … they'd …"

He stopped here, an angry scowl coming across his face.

"You don't have to go on right now," Chloe said.

"No … I don't mind. It's just … everything I can tell you is going to only make me look more and more like the killer."

"We can have—"

"They'd strip me down naked, push me against the wall, and pretend to rape me. They made a huge theatrical thing out of it. On one occasion, after a victory, Bo Luntz used the capped end of a shampoo bottle to penetrate me. And that was the moment... the moment I became nothing but a piñata to those assholes. There were a few times where someone would pin me down on the floor and a few of them would take turns putting their privates in my face. Slapping me on the cheeks with them... spitting on me..."

Chloe felt as if someone had sucked all of the air out of the room. "And you never told anyone?"

"I told the coach. And he apparently had a talk with a few of the guys because after that, whenever they had a chance, they'd threaten my life. Called me a faggot, a tattletale. Bo Luntz said if I opened my mouth again, he'd use a broom handle rather than a shampoo bottle."

Matt Sawyer was crying now, his voice wavering as he wiped tears away. The timing of the break in his speech was perfect, though. As he wiped the tears away, the door to the office opened. Rhodes stepped in, looking confused and pissed off.

She looked back and forth between Chloe and Sawyer. With a scowl on her face, she sat down beside Chloe and looked across the table at Sawyer.

"Mr. Sawyer, this is my partner, Agent Rhodes."

Rhodes nodded her acknowledgment but said nothing. Chloe could feel the tension coming off of her and she knew they were going to have to have a talk before they went any farther on this case. First, of course, there was the issue of Matt Sawyer.

"Agent Rhodes," Chloe said, trying to sound as professional as possible. "Mr. Sawyer knew the three victims in high school. He has just finished telling me how he was severely bullied by them. And I don't expect him to have to explain it again."

"Much appreciated," Sawyer said, just now getting back his composure.

"I will note, though, Mr. Sawyer, that everything you just described to me *does* only strengthen the case against you."

"I understand that. But that was forty years ago. I've been to therapy. I'm married and have two amazing daughters. Who the hell would hold on to that sort of a grudge for so long?"

"Someone, apparently," Rhodes said.

"I have nothing to hold a grudge against. I went on to do very well for myself. At the risk of sounding like an absolute prick, I'd be comfortable saying that my life was much better than theirs. And I was aware of this...I have been for quite some time. *That* was my revenge against them. And yes, I'll admit...a huge part of my drive during college was to make sure I did better than every single one of them."

"Could you give us alibis for where you have been over the course of the past week or so?"

"I'd have to give you a pretty long list of people, but yes. If that's what you need to take me off of the list of suspects, I can do that for you."

"Thank you," Chloe said. "All things considered, you've been very cooperative."

Before Sawyer could say anything else, Rhodes leaned over. In not quite a whisper, she said: "Can we speak outside, please?"

"Mr. Sawyer, could you give us a moment?" Chloe said as she got to her feet.

She and Rhodes walked out into the hallway, Rhodes closing the office door behind them. For a moment, Chloe thought she was going to get a glimpse of that older version of Rhodes, the bad ass that dared people to get in her way. Chloe almost *wanted* to see it. But, while Rhodes was clearly mad, she remained calm as she leaned against the wall.

"So what the hell is going on?" Rhodes asked.

"I know you may not believe it, but I *am* sorry. But last night after our little argument, I just couldn't stop. And maybe it *is* because of all of Danielle's drama and my father. But I ended up meeting with Angie Wells. She told me some things she remembered about Richard, which led me to Matt Sawyer. He was the football team's water boy and based on everything he just told me, they abused him terribly."

Chloe watched Rhodes go through a few different facial expressions. Chloe was interested to see if she'd hone in on the fact that she, Chloe, had kept working the case without her or if she wanted to skip over all of that and focus on the case.

"You think he did it?"

"He *is* small statured, like the coroner suggested. But I don't know… he doesn't really fit the mold, but I can't be sure. We just need to get his alibis and see if they hold up."

"Then let's do that," Rhodes said.

"Just like that? Are we cool?"

"I think we will be. I'd like to talk some things over with you when this case is all wrapped up. And I'd also appreciate not being left out of any interviews from here on out."

"Fair enough," Chloe said.

Rhodes nodded and opened the door to the office again. When they stepped back in, Matt Sawyer was going through his phone, copying and pasting a few contacts into a text message.

"What are you doing?" Chloe asked.

"Giving you a list of people that I worked with over the last week or so. I'm sure you understand, I'd like to have this behind me so I can get back to work as soon as possible."

"Of course," Chloe said.

"Mr. Sawyer," Rhodes said, "are there any others you can think of who would have had reasons to hold grudges against these men?"

"Just about anyone who wasn't in their little social circle," Sawyer said. "They were particularly terrible to me, but they were just flat out rude to anyone they wanted to. If you were looking for everyone they had ever wronged, you'd be busy for the rest of the year."

Chloe sighed and folded her arms. "Send me that list," she said, nodding to his phone. "We'll try to get you out of here as soon as possible."

With that, she gave Sawyer her number so he could text her the list. He was right; it was quite extensive. And if past cases has taught her anything, it was that people who could provide alibi lists this long and detailed tended to be innocent.

"You know who else you might want to look into, if you don't mind me making the suggestion?" Sawyer said.

"Who?" Rhodes asked.

"The coach of the team. Dick Yancy. Probably the worst teacher in my school. Creeped al the girls out and, from what I've heard recently, was eventually fired because of some sort of misconduct or another."

"Do you know if he's local?"

"Oh sure. Holed up in some old folks home last I heard."

The smile on Sawyer's face was a little too wide. Apparently, he was indeed getting all the revenge he needed in seeing how those who had tormented him in the past—and those associated with them—were playing out their later years.

"Thanks for the tip," Chloe said. "Give us a few minutes."

She left the room, with Rhodes behind her, seeking out another room to place the calls to Sawyer's co-workers and family. But even before the first one was placed, she felt that he was likely innocent. He had come along too freely, and had a list of alibis eight people deep.

Still, they now had the high school football team as a link. And if Chloe had learned anything in high school—especially as the weird girl with a dead mom and an incarcerated father—it was that high schoolers could be downright cruel.

CHAPTER NINETEEN

It took less than half an hour to clear Matt Sawyer. Two of his fellow real estate agents had even offered to send over copies of the agency's register which would provide times and dates when Sawyer had shown houses. His wife, while a little pissed that her husband had even been considered a suspect at all, had volunteered the phone numbers of another local couple they had enjoyed a cookout with on the very same afternoon Bo Luntz had been murdered.

But even as they had let Sawyer go, his mood a little flustered but all around unbothered for the most part, Chloe did not let herself feel overwhelmed or defeated. If she went there, she'd start thinking about Danielle. For now, she had to look ahead. She had to be a good agent—and a better partner to Rhodes.

Looking ahead meant meeting with Richard "Dick" Yancy. He had been easy enough to locate. Rhodes had done a search for local hospice and elderly care centers under the name Dick Yancy, getting an instant result. One phone call later and they were on the way to Everwood Retirement Village just twenty minutes after releasing Matt Sawyer.

When they checked in at the front desk, the woman behind the computer gave them a wary glance as she gave them Yancy's room number, even after seeing their IDs. Chloe supposed she understood. No one was going to look favorably upon two federal agents who were about to question an eighty-one-year-old man who had to live out the last of his days in hospice—especially not someone who worked for the home.

"We know nothing about Mr. Yancy," Chloe told the woman behind the computer. "His name simply came up in an investigation as a potential resource. Can you please tell us what to expect so we can structure the questions accordingly?"

The woman seemed to warm at the question, if only slightly. She sighed and looked back and forth between Chloe and Rhodes before answering. "He's just very weak, really. He beat cancer last year but the chemo and the treatments just took it out of him. He also has a nerve disorder that makes it difficult for him to walk. Because of that, he doesn't really care to try to get active. He's very depressed most days, to be honest. He's physically sort of a mess but the old man sure does have a mind as sharp as a tack."

"Thank you," Rhodes said.

"We will do our best to be as easygoing and non-confrontational as possible," Chloe added.

The woman nodded, already picking up her phone as the agents headed away. *Probably calling the manager to let them know that federal agents are about to question one of their residents,* Chloe thought.

As they walked down the long corridor that led to the recreational area, Chloe found Everwood Retirement Village to be a much nicer place than she had been expecting. Granted, she had only ever been in one retirement home before, and it had been an absolute dump compared to Everwood.

The rec area was a large and brightly colored room, set up with several tables, chairs, and plush furniture. There were four older women sitting around a table, playing a card game. Other residents were spread out, either watching a movie together on the wall-mounted television, or reading in various little reading nooks located throughout the room.

They found Dick Yancy's room down a hallway to the left of the rec room. The door was partially opened; Chloe could hear the murmur of a television from inside. She knocked on the door and was greeted with a rather gruff-sounding *"Yeah, come in in!"*

Chloe and Rhodes entered the room slowly, not sure what to expect. Chloe found a man sitting in an armchair against the left

wall, his legs kicked up. He was watching something on a laptop—
football highlights of some kind or another if the voiceover she was
hearing was any indication. He was very thin, and his eyes looked
sunken in. But when he looked up at them, there was alertness and
awareness in his eyes. And the smile on his face showed the ghost of
the handsome man he had once been.

"Are you Mr. Yancy?" Chloe asked.

"Yeah, that's me. And who are you?"

"I'm Agent Chloe Fine, with the FBI. This is my partner, Agent
Rhodes."

"FBI?" he said with a chuckle. "What on earth for?" He paused
whatever he had been looking at and closed the screen. He then
habitually messed with his mop of gray hair, as if trying to smooth
it down.

"Well, we're investigating three murders and have recently discovered a link between them all. That link just happens to be that
they all played football for the Summit Hills Cougars during one of
the championship years, back in the late eighties."

"Oh my God," Yancy said. The surprised look almost stalled
on his face, as if his mind could not quite comprehend it. "Which
players?"

"Bo Luntz, Richard Wells, and Gordon Nettles."

Chloe could see the recognition dawning on his face. He
frowned, the bottom right corner of his mouth ticking in a nervous
way. "How recent?"

"In the last week or so," Chloe said. "All three of them."

Yancy nodded, removing the laptop from his legs and setting
it on the arm of the couch. As he sat up, Chloe could truly see just
how fragile the man seemed.

"Mr. Yancy," Rhodes said, "can you tell us what you remember about those men in particular? Maybe about the team as a
whole?"

"Yes, yes…well, I won three state championships, but only
one of them with that team. I know the names, sure, and I can
almost see some of the faces. But…I don't know that I can recall

the positions. Though I think Nettles...I think he was a halfback. Luntz...a receiver, maybe? I can't recall."

"Do you remember any of them getting into any sort of trouble?" Chloe asked.

He took a moment to think about it and then shook his head after about ten seconds or so. He looked rather disappointed. "If they did, it was nothing I ever heard about." There was a dim little sparkle in his eyes and his memories took him back. "My God, that was a great team. Undefeated. And I believe the quarterback threw for thirty-one touchdowns with just five interceptions—a record at that time, you know...and he didn't even finish out the season."

"And none of them had any issues with others in the school?" Rhodes asked. "No fights or disciplinary actions of any kind?"

"I can't remember any from Nettles, Luntz, or Wells. But...now, that quarterback—Brock Mason was his name—he got into some trouble. Like I said, he didn't finish out the season. Not because of an injury or anything like that...but because he made some stupid choices."

"Like what?" Chloe asked.

"Drugs, if I remember correctly. He also got caught with a young lady in the boys' bathroom, doing certain...well, you know...And he had a temper on him, too. Made quite the scene in the principal's office a few times if I remember correctly."

"How did the other players react to him being booted from the team?"

"They were pissed, of course. But not at me. That was a decision the school board made, not me...just a lowly old coach. But they got over it pretty quickly. We managed to narrowly pull out a win at the championship with the second-string QB."

"Did any of the players ever give *you* any trouble?" Chloe asked.

"None at all. Now, I will admit...they did get rambunctious. Every team I've ever had did, though. You get that many boys, throw in some adrenaline and a competitive sport, and it's just going to happen."

"Did anyone from the school ever come to you with complaints?"

"Oh, all the time. Sometimes the boys would moon people as they made their way out of the school grounds on the buses to go to other schools to play. Every now and then we got reports of some of our players sort of bullying freshmen. Things like that. But usually all it took was a stern talking to and they would straighten up."

"There was nothing you can think of that might have been beyond the line? Maybe something even unforgivable?"

He thought for a moment, his eyes cast downward. Chloe studied him closely, fully expecting him to say something. "No. I will say that there are many regrets... things I would have done differently for my boys. But no... I can think of nothing that would have crossed a line."

Chloe wanted to push harder on this but the old man looked fragile. Besides that, even if there *was* something, she wasn't sure how clearly or accurately Yancy would remember it.

Chloe was growing more and more certain with every answer they got that even if there *had* been something vile going on during the time Lunt, Wells, and Nettles had played for Yancy, he'd had no idea. In his old age, he had chosen to remember only the nice things. Also, he had coached in a time when roughhousing boys tended to get away with quite a lot if they were on a winning football team.

Besides, she felt like they may have landed a nugget of useful information. Brock Mason, the quarterback who had gotten kicked off the team. Surely he had some negative memories of the team. If there was dirt on the team and its players, surely he'd have it.

"Do you happen to know if Brock Mason still lives in the area?" Chloe asked.

"Sadly, I don't. I haven't spoken to any of my old players in years." His eyes grew distant here, either dozing out or focusing on some past memory that he could not quite rope down.

"Mr. Yancy, thank you very much for your time," Chloe said.

"Of course," he said. "It was nice to have visitors. I wish I could have been more help to you."

"Oh, this was fine," Rhodes said. "Just... please, if you think of anything else that might help us find the person who killed these men, please let one of the doctors or assistants know so they can get in touch with us."

"I will," Yancy said. But he still had that faraway look in his eyes. Chloe felt for him; he was swept up in memories of the past—memories that were likely the best he'd had and were the best he was ever going to get.

They made their way out of Yancy's room and back down toward the lobby. They weren't outside of Yancy's room for a total of five seconds before Chloe took out her phone and dialed up Anderson. He answered fairly quickly, apparently just as eager to wrap this case as they were.

"Agent Fine, what have you got for me?"

"Nothing yet. I do have a name that I'd like you to run for me. I need an address, phone number, and criminal history if there is one."

"Sure thing. Let me know what you need and I'll work my magic over here."

She gave him Brock Mason's name and was told he would call her back within ten minutes. Yet, much to her surprise and delight, she saw his number pop back up on her caller display when her phone rang just as she was backing out of the Everwood Retirement Village parking lot.

"That was quick," Chloe said as she answered the call.

"Well, it was easy to find. Brock Mason…he's been quite the busy and notorious fellow. I'm looking at two possession of illegal substance charges, one charge of intent to sell, a few contempt of courts, a DUI, and an assault charge that was knocked down to a misdemeanor."

"Is he still local?"

"Oh yeah. Lives downtown. Looking at his record, he spent about a week in jail less than three months ago for one of these possession charges. I'll send you over the address."

"Thanks, Anderson."

"Hey, thank you, guys. The two of you are a pretty efficient machine."

She chuckled, though the comment made her cringe. She knew that she and Rhodes worked very well together. It was why she felt so much guilt about the way she had behaved the night before.

She ended the call and looked over at Rhodes. "Look…I went off the rails last night. My personal stuff isn't—"

"Chloe. Shut up. We're good."

Chloe gave a smile and returned her focus to the road, pointing them toward the downtown district.

CHAPTER TWENTY

Brock Mason actually lived in a rather confusing section of downtown that was just far enough away from the business section and close enough to the run-down section to still be considered downtown. His rented townhome was tucked away in a shoddy development—the sort that looks like a seedy motel rather than a collection of townhomes if you drive by it fast enough.

As Chloe parked, she also discovered that it was the type of development where the residents tended to lounge around on their stoops on Sunday afternoons. As Chloe and Rhodes made their way to Mason's townhouse, Choe counted at least two different men—both appearing to be in middle age—leering unapologetically at them. One of them whistled at her—a tactic she had always thought was strange. Did men really think women would respond to such idiocy?

"I think that was for me," Rhodes said with a lopsided grin.

"Oh, you can have it."

They approached Mason's townhouse, the second to last on the backside of the U-shaped development. A single car was parked somewhat crookedly in the space outside of the place. They stepped up onto the concrete slab of a porch together, Rhodes knocking and taking a single step back. As they waited, Chloe looked around behind them. It was the sort of place that just seemed to give off bad vibes (not that she believed in vibes). What she did believe in, though, was her instinct. And her instincts told her that was likely the type of place the police visited at least once every weekend.

When no one came to the door within twenty seconds, Rhodes knocked again, much harder this time. Her knocking echoed softly through the court of concrete and grass, attracting the attention of a few who were just sitting around.

This time, Rhodes got a response. A wavering but deep, *"Hold on already!"*

The sound of shuffling feet came to the door. There was a slight clicking sound and then a fumbling noise as the doorknob was toyed with on the other side. When it finally opened, the man on the other side looked like he might very well fall right through the doorway and onto the porch. He seemed to catch himself at the last moment, propping himself up against the doorframe.

He's high as a damned kite, Chloe thought. She wasn't sure what he was on, but the glaze in his eyes and the almost desperate way he tried to push himself away from the doorframe so he could stand on his own helped her narrow it down to a few choice drugs.

"Yeah?" he asked, looking at both of them and trying his best to try on a charming smile.

"Are you Brock Mason?" Rhodes asked.

He seemed to think about it for a moment. He looked over their shoulders, out into the court between the two rows of townhouses. There was a dreamlike quality to the way he stared, but it was a very focused stare all the same. His eyes were moving quickly around and the pupils of his blue eyes were dilated.

It's probably meth, Chloe thought. If she was correct, she knew he'd either be languid and useless the entire time, or that he could be a big box of mood swings. Either way, she thought they might still be able to get some information out of him. It was her experience that when speaking to high people, they often did not have much of a filter when it came to revealing too much information.

"Yeah, that's me," he finally said. "Who're you?"

"We're Agents Rhodes and Fine," Chloe said, showing her ID. Mason stared at it long and hard, blinking almost comically as his eyes tried to focus on it. "We were wondering if you had time to talk."

Chloe saw fear try to gather in his eyes but whatever he was on made it hard for the emotion to truly register. She could see him trying to work something out, but it just wouldn't click.

"Nah, sorry, I don't have much to say. I can—"

"We're fully aware of your criminal record," Chloe said. "Rest assured, we are not here about any of that. This is about an entirely different matter. We just need to ask you a few questions about some men you might have known."

Again, he looked like he was struggling to keep up with the chain of events taking place directly in front of him.

"Nah, I'm not gonna talk to you."

"I don't recall giving you a choice in the matter," Rhodes said. "So you either talk to us right now, like civil people, or we can make a scene in front of your neighbors. It's clear you're high off your ass … and I have no issue using that to my advantage. Got it?"

Mason backed up a step and reached for the door. But he then seemed to think better of it. He tottered on his feet again and then looked them over one more time. "What's this … what the questions about?"

Yeah, meth for sure, Chloe thought. *He can't get a sentence out and his eyes are moving so fast, it's like he's trying to watch a tennis match.* His thin body stature almost indicated that meth was his go-to drug.

"You going to invite us in?" Rhodes asked.

He shook his head and tried on his charming grin again. "You'd like that, huh?" He snickered at this comment and then stepped out onto the porch, leaving the door wide open behind him.

"We need to ask you some questions about a few men you went to high school with," Chloe said. "We understand you were the quarterback for the Summit Hills Cougars."

"'S right," Mason said proudly. "Championship year. Won state."

"But you didn't finish the year out, did you?" Rhodes asked. Chloe cringed inside. She was really letting Mason have it.

"So what?" he asked, indignant. "Get outta here with that shit. You … you want me to answer questions or what?"

"Mr. Mason, do you remember a man by the name of Matt Sawyer?" Rhodes asked.

He nodded, the smile faltering from his face. "What you need to know about him for?"

"Can you just answer the question?" Chloe asked.

"No. I paid for all that. It ate at me for a long time, you know? I'm not talking about that. You two…just fuck off, yeah?"

"Mr. Mason, calm down," Chloe said. "We're trying to keep this civil."

His mood shifted so quickly that it was almost like watching someone slip a mask over his face. If there had been any amusement or interest behind those dilated pupils, it was replaced by defensiveness and rage.

"I'm not talking about any of that," he said, nearly screaming it.

"Mr. Mason," Rhodes said, her back going rigid as she planted her feet firmly. Chloe could see her partner getting into a subtle defensive posture, ready for whatever might happen next. "I will tell you this. Your name has come up as someone linked to three men that were recently murdered. The more you give us trouble and refuse to help, the more—"

"I'm done with all of that!"

Mason screamed this, almost like a child throwing a tantrum. And as he ended the statement, he reached out and tried to shove Rhodes. Rhodes, however, was not only ready, but was much faster. She brushed the shove away with ease, simply throwing out her right arm in a sweeping motion. As Mason was pushed to the side from the force of the block, Rhodes responded in kind.

She shoved him hard enough to have him stumble back into the side of the house. When he rebounded and came back toward her, Rhodes took him in a headlock and dropped to the ground. The entire ordeal lasted less than three seconds. Chloe followed it all with precision, already there with the handcuffs when Rhodes went to her knees.

Mason grunted and squealed in Rhodes's grip while Chloe cuffed him. Several people sitting out in the court were applauding and laughing.

"Sorry about that," Rhodes whispered.

Chloe smiled and shook her head. "You handled it better than I would have. I would have decked him."

"To your feet, Mr. Mason," Rhodes said, jerking him back up and grabbing him by his right arm. "Looks like we're going to be spending a good deal of time in an interrogation room."

Chloe looked to Mason and saw the fear in his eyes again. She wasn't quite ready to say it was the product of guilt, though. If anything, somewhere beyond the haze of the meth, he seemed to start understanding the ramifications of what he had just done—attacking an FBI agent might be just about the dumbest thing to go on his record.

Chloe and Rhodes escorted Brock Mason down to their car to the cheering and laughter of Mason's neighbors. It was a strange sound and an even stranger feeling because as much as Chloe hated to admit it, the applause lifted her spirits a bit as they drove back toward the Central District with a potential killer in tow.

CHAPTER TWENTY ONE

Because of his attack on Rhodes, there was no question that Mason was going to spend some time behind bars—even if just another slap-on-the-wrist sentence of a few weeks or so. Due to this, Brock Mason spent about an hour going through the post-arrest process of getting his mugshot taken, being processed into the system again, fingerprints, and so on. The lag was fine with Chloe; it gave her and Rhodes some time to regroup after the unexpected chain of events, and gave Mason an hour to come around out of his drug-fueled stupor.

While they waited, Chloe and Rhodes looked over Mason's record. It was exactly as Anderson had suggested, although Anderson had left out of some the minor details. For instance, the assault charge that had been dropped down to a misdemeanor had been filed by an ex-girlfriend. The assault had blackened an eye and broken two fingers on her left hand. As for the substance-related charges, they all seemed to make sense and fit with his profile.

When Mason was fully processed, he was escorted into an interrogation room. Chloe and Rhodes didn't give him much time to get acclimated to the situation before they also entered the room. Chloe could recall that fresh, still-wet blood at the scene of Gordon Nettles's murder. It reminded her just how close behind the killer they had been—and where they were currently.

When Chloe sat down in one of the chairs on the opposite side of the interrogation table, she saw a little less of that faraway haze in Mason's eyes. Now he looked tired and irritated. There was another look on his face that Chloe had seen multiple times before in rooms just like this: the look of a man who knew he had done something very stupid and was not quite ready to face up to it just yet.

"You remember why you're here?" Chloe asked. She was very aware of Rhodes, standing behind her. Rhodes rarely sat when they were in interrogation rooms together, but Chloe did not know if it was her own personal preference or if Rhodes was, by nature, rather fidgety and could not sit still.

"Yeah," Brock said. "I didn't mean to ..."

He looked up at Rhodes as a means to finish his statement without actually saying it.

"Well, you were rather stoned out of your mind," Chloe pointed out.

He shrugged. He looked defeated; he knew this particular visit to the precinct might turn out to be much worse than any of his previous visits.

"Drug charges aside," Chloe said, "do you recall why Agent Rhodes and I came knocking on your door in the first place?"

"You asked me if I remembered Matt Sawyer."

"That's right. And that name seemed to set you off. You said you had moved beyond that ... that you were trying to put those parts of your past behind you."

"I have. I was a miserable little shit back then. Maybe I still am, I don't know. But yeah ... I did some things to Matt Sawyer that I am definitely not proud of."

"You didn't act alone, though, did you?" Rhodes asked. She stepped closer to the table, her arms crossed and her eyes fixed tightly on Mason's face.

Something seemed to dawn on Mason—not worry, but not relief, either. He slowly shook his head and answered, "No. There were a few of us. Mean little shits ... four or five of us."

"What were their names?"

Chloe watched him closely as he answered. She had her own hunch that Mason was likely not the killer. First of all, they were likely looking for someone of smaller stature and Mason easily stood at six feet or a little over. He also had fairly muscular arms and shoulders that stood in opposition against his scrawny frame. Lastly, someone addicted to meth was likely not the sort of person who could enter a home, kill someone, and then leave—all without leaving a single trace of evidence ... save for the socks shoved down the throats of the victims.

When he gave a few names, it basically confirmed that he was not the killer. Or, if he *was* the killer, was simply quite dumb for giving them the names so easily.

"Bo Luntz was one. Guy named Gordon Nettles was another. There was one or two more but ... I don't know? I don't even remember them."

"Are you certain?" Chloe asked. She had been hoping for this; if he could give the names of others involved, it might help them to prevent anyone else from being killed.

"Yeah, hell, I don't remember much of anything from high school anymore." He said it sadly, as if he feared there might be some memories worth salvaging.

"But you remember some of the things you did to Matt Sawyer?" Rhodes asked.

He nodded firmly. "Yeah ... because it sort of drilled itself into my head. I might try to change but some things ... well, they stay there whether you want them to or not."

"You'll probably be here for a while," Chloe said. "I want you to spend that time thinking about some of the other guys that bullied Matt Sawyer."

"What's the big deal about Sawyer, anyway?" Mason asked.

Before Chloe could give him an answer, her phone rang. Typically, she would have ignored it but the moment she heard the tone and felt it vibrating, her thoughts instantly turned to Danielle.

"One second," she said. When she turned away from Mason, she briefly faced Rhodes. She gave Rhodes a sad and pleading look, to which Rhodes simply nodded.

Chloe stepped out into the hallway and grabbed instantly at her phone. The number on the display was not a saved one, but it did have a DC area code. She answered it on the third ring, a little spark of hope firing off in her chest.

"This is Agent Fine," she answered.

"Agent Fine, this is Detective Graves, the detective looking into your sister's disappearance. We met briefly at your father's townhouse?"

"Yes, I remember. What have you found?"

That spark of hope seemed to ricochet around, not sure if was viable or not. But Chloe *had* to hope. Because the only other emotion she could conjure up was dread and she could not put herself through that. Not right now.

"I just wanted to check in with you," he said. "I'm afraid I don't have any news. We've checked your father's place, your sister's place, even spoken to some people where your sister works. We're stuck at zero. No leads, no witnesses, no evidence…nothing."

The first thought that went through her head was: *Then why the hell are you even calling?* But that was pushed aside by the realization that he was calling as a courtesy. He knew she had been worried and wanted to keep her updated—even if there was really nothing to update.

"So call in the State PD," she ventured. But she knew how the whole process worked and just how illogical that would be. If there was more evidence, it would be more likely. But as it stood, the case to find Danielle was just about as dead in the water as her current case to find the killer of three high school football players.

"Agent, you know how that's going to fly this early on. We have nothing to present to them. A worried sister, two missing people— who are related to one another, mind you—and a tiny smear of blood on a teakettle. If we don't get any hits within another few days, sure…we'll likely call the State. But for now…"

"I know, I know," she said. She swallowed down a deep sigh and said: "Thanks for letting me know. Please continue to keep me updated."

She ended the call before Detective Graves had a chance to say anything else. She instantly turned back to the interrogation room door but paused before her hand could fall on it. The phone call had derailed her, sent her thoughts crashing back down to Danielle. And given the lackluster dead ends she and Rhodes were finding over and over again on this current case, that was the worst thing that could happen.

As she finally willed herself to enter the interrogation room again, she felt quite certain that if Brock Mason turned out to not be their killer, they were going to soon be faced with a fourth vic-tim—possibly by the end of the day, if the killer's schedule and speed to this point were any indication.

CHAPTER TWENTY TWO

Forty-eight hours.

Those words—that number—kept pulsing in Chloe's mind like a drumbeat. Even after Mason had given them two alibis that, if they turned out truthful, would clear him of the deaths of Nettles and Wells, her mind remained locked on that number.

Forty-eight. Forty-eight hours.

She'd done enough research and had read about enough cases to know that after forty-eight hours, the chance of finding a missing person becomes infinitely smaller. It was this reality that had her sitting in a bathroom stall of the Central District station, finally allowing herself to weep. The reality that she might not ever see her sister again was starting to seep into every thought. Following the call from Detective Graves, she'd only remained in the interrogation room for five minutes before she'd had to step out. She was not going to cry in front of Rhodes and she damn sure wasn't going to lose it in front of Brock Mason. So as Mason was telling them about where he had been the previous afternoon while Gordon Nettles was being killed, Chloe had excused herself rushed to the restroom, and locked herself inside.

She wasn't sure how long she had been sitting in the stall. She had finally started to get control of herself, no longer sobbing and sniffing in wet breaths. She wanted to make sure it was all behind her before she stepped out, wanted to—

The bathroom door opened and a woman started walking into the bathroom. The footfalls stopped after a few seconds. There was a pause and then Rhodes's voice.

"Fine?"

Chloe froze for a moment but then realize that this was likely going to be the moment that would determine their future as partners. They were going to be vulnerable or they were going to be distant. And really, Rhodes had already done her part. She had come after her, knowing full well why she had stepped out.

So now it was up to Chloe to make that next move. With a sigh, she got up from the closed toilet lid, unlocked the door, and stepped out. Fortunately, they were the only two in the restroom.

"Sorry about that," Chloe said.

"No need to be. I wanted to make sure you were okay."

"I'm … well, no. Honestly, no. I'm a mess. I know Johnson was right … that me staying home would have driven me crazy. But Rhodes … I can't *not* think about it."

"I won't even pretend to imagine what you're going through. But what I *can* do is offer you this nugget: Brock Mason actually gave me a damned good idea. He said we could see all of the popular football jocks by just looking through his yearbook. Said they all signed it and scrawled crude notes on it."

"Does he actually have it at his home?" Chloe asked.

"He says he doesn't think so. He lost it somewhere in one of about ten moves over the past twenty years. But I asked one of the officers on duty for the number to the high school, hoping they might have a copy archived or something. When I told him what I needed, he introduced me to another officer—a local, been here all his life. He graduated two years after Mason and all of his buddies, but he does have the yearbook from the year the team won the state championship. He left about five minutes ago to drive out to his house to get it."

"That's great news."

They stood there a moment longer, and Chloe knew that Rhodes was not going to budge until she, Chloe, did so. Rhodes was trying to make sure her partner did not want to further discuss what had brought her rushing to the bathroom—what had kept her on edge and out of sorts for the last thirty-six hours or so.

"Thanks for handling Mason while I had my breakdown," Chloe said, heading for the door.

"My pleasure," Rhodes said.

"With Mason? Pleasure? Really?"

"Oh, for sure. He had this look on his face like he was afraid I might toss him around again."

Chloe managed a laugh, but it was painfully fake. But it was enough to break the awkwardness of the moment as she and Rhodes left the restroom and headed back toward their makeshift office.

They had the yearbook in their possession twenty minutes later and wasted no time going through it. Chloe turned to the back of the book, where the teams were located. It came as no surprise that the football team was pictured first. Together, she and Rhodes studied the picture, circling the faces of the recently murdered, as well as Brock Mason. It was slightly eerie to be staring at the young faces— a team before the start of the season that had no idea they were only a few months away from winning a state championship.

Standing to the back and all the way to the right, nearly hidden by an offensive lineman, was Matt Sawyer, who looked very much the same as the man they had spoken to earlier in the day. There were a few other pictures of the team in practice. Several of them showed team members without their helmets, chatting on the sideline. Another showed a few members taking part in a parade. In two of these, Bo Luntz and Richard Wells could be seen side by side.

"I still don't quite understand how we can identify a killer based on old high school pictures," Rhodes said.

"Well, with three players now dead—players we are pretty sure participated in the bullying of Matt Sawyer—I'm thinking the killer maybe wasn't a popular kid. I think the killer might be another Matt Sawyer."

"So someone that was bullied…someone with something to prove."

"I think so. And I also think the fact that Brock Mason has not been killed proves that. If any players had reason to hate these other players, what would it be? Maybe losing games? Or even something like taking a position and knocking them down to second string. Something like that. I'd think if the killer was a part of the team, they would have gone after the troublemaker first."

"A troublemaker like Brock Mason," Rhodes said. "The star quarterback that could have easily cost them their season."

"Exactly."

"But that could be anyone," Rhodes pointed out. "And there are a lot of kids in this book."

"So we need a big net. We'll have to get the bureau's tech team on it. See if we can get some help here from the local PD."

"To what? Get information on every student in this book?" Rhodes's tone indicated she thought this was a massive task to take on. Chloe knew it was, too. But for right now, she did not see that they had any other options.

"I think we can start with just the males, and we can eliminate the freshmen for now. Given what we know about Matt Sawyer and the type of abuse they doled out, I doubt it would be anyone who was not affiliated with the football team. And it was the varsity team, meaning freshmen would not be involved at all."

Having narrowed the field down significantly, it appeared that Rhodes was a bit more agreeable. She was nodded as she turned quickly through the pages. "I can call this in to DC if you can speak to someone here at the station. It might be quicker if I just take pictures of each page and send it like that. It'll save a trip back and forth to DC."

"Great idea," Chloe said.

Rhodes didn't say anything in agreement and that was fine with Chloe. It *was* a huge task, one that was going to take far too long. But if it was the one potential source of viable information they had, they needed to run with it however they could. But even then, with this little hope blooming, Chloe thought of how Sherry Luntz and Angie Wells had talked about their friends, and even friends who would become future husbands, who had moved around a bit. And if there were students in this yearbook who had moved from somewhere else and *they* happened to be the killer, they could easily fly under the radar.

But that was a worry for another time. For now, they had to work along the road they had been given, no matter how wide and endless it seemed.

CHAPTER TWENTY THREE

Even after eliminating all females in the Summit Hills yearbook from that year, as well as all freshmen, that still left two hundred and eleven males to search. Slowly, even that number dwindled down. A few had died, a few had moved to other countries, and so on. After eliminations like this, the number was knocked down to one hundred and ninety-three within just half an hour.

There were currently three FBI resource agents assisting with the project, as well as Detective Anderson, two police officers, and Chloe and Rhodes. It was monotonous work that made Chloe feel as if they were wasting their time, but she was surprised to find just how quickly they were able to go through the names. But even as they were able to find information about some of the names as well as eliminating quite a few of them, Chloe could not help but feel as if it was a complete and utter waste of time.

For about two hours, it was as if she was part of some strange call center. Anderson helped set her up at a desk with a precinct phone, creating a makeshift office. She'd choose a name from the yearbook that had been assigned to her (names had been broken up into groups of thirty among each person taking part in the task), run a search within the precinct's database, and determine whether or not the person was worth placing a call to. In the space of that two hours, she had called eight potential leads and suspects, weeding them out based on alibis that she wrote down to check on.

Just as she felt that she was reaching her breaking point, Anderson came to the door. He stepped into the room with a single sheet of paper, a few notes scribbled on it in his long and leaning handwriting.

"I've got a guy by the name of Wade Stephenson. He's a local, but moved away after high school. Went to college, lived in Maine for a while...that is, up until about three weeks ago. He works as an accountant and got a better job in Baltimore. His current home address is about forty minutes away from Gordon Nettles's home."

"Any run-ins with our bullies back in high school?"

"He clammed up about that when he was asked. The call was made by one of the local officers and I was listening in. He got really defensive, said he didn't want to talk about it, but we could maybe call later. I got the impression he was at work. We pushed him a bit, but he was adamant."

"Where does he work?" Chloe asked.

"Got the address right here," Anderson said, shaking the paper.

"Awesome work," she said, taking it from him. She and Rhodes were already getting to their feet, scooping up the case files and their cell phones.

"Should I keep everyone looking into the rest of the names?"

"I hate to say it, but probably," Chloe said. "I'd rather have all the bases covered. Plus, let's bump the people we know once played on that championship team to the top of the list. We can only assume they might be next on the killer's list. Maybe give them something of a heads-up."

Anderson gave a little mock salute and then headed back the way he had come. He seemed almost a little saddened that he wouldn't be going out with them. She nearly asked him to come along, but three authority figures questioning an attorney about his involvement (or lack thereof) in a series of murders might make Mr. Stephenson reluctant to talk.

She and Rhodes rushed out to their car, Rhodes already plugging the address into the GPS on her phone. It made Chloe think of another potential resource, so she also pulled out her phone as she got behind the wheel. She went to her previous calls and selected Angie Wells as she started the car.

She wasn't too terribly surprised when Angie answered right away. The funeral had just ended a few hours ago, so she was likely looking for anything to take her mind off of it. At least, that's the vibe Chloe had gotten from her when they'd spoken at the hotel bar. It was, as it turned out, apparently a correct hunch.

"Jesus, what is it now?" Angie Wells asked.

"I have one question about another potential lead or suspect," Chloe said. "If you'd rather just be done with this, say so right now and I'll hang up. I know today had to be hard on you."

"What's the question?" Angie asked, clearly irritated but also rather accommodating.

"I'm headed to find a man named Wade Stephenson. Does that name mean anything to you?"

"Yeah," Angie said, without giving it much thought. "He was another of the victims of all of the stupid bullying. I don't think he ever got it quite as bad Matt Sawyer, but he got some of it, all right. I think Stephenson was the one who tried out for the team, almost made it as kicker, I think. He might have even made it on the team but got cut after pre-season scrimmages. I *think* it was him. There was a story going around about some guys on the team shoving him inside of a locker in the changing room and locking him in there."

"But you're not certain it was him?"

"No, but I'm pretty sure it was him. But I *do* know that he got the brunt of a lot of other mean-spirited things. Shoving him against lockers between classes, just to embarrass him, you know? I think it was Wade that somebody—Bo Luntz, maybe—dumped a lunch tray of spaghetti on his head right in the middle of the cafeteria, in front of everyone."

"Anything else?"

"Nothing specific that I can remember, no."

"Okay. Thanks again, Ms. Wells."

"Sure. Are you ... well, are you any closer?"

"I'm hoping so," Chloe said, well aware of how vague of an answer she was giving.

Angie said nothing else. She simply ended the call, the click of it filling Chloe's head. Before she could let it affect her, she turned to Rhodes and said: "We got directions?"

"We do," she said, and told her where to go.

When they walked into Stephenson and Jenkins Accounting a little more than half an hour later, they entered as quickly as they could while also trying not to appear as if they were in a rush. If Stephenson was indeed a very likely candidate for the killer—or, for that matter, for a potential victim—they didn't want to scare him right away.

There was a young man sitting at a desk inside of a small lobby as they entered. He looked straight out of college and overly eager to help them when they entered.

"We need to speak with Wade Stephenson," Chloe said. "It's quite urgent."

"Oh, I'm afraid he stepped out just a bit ago."

"Do you know how long ago?" Rhodes asked.

"I'm afraid not. Fifteen minutes, maybe? Certainly no more than half an hour ago."

"Did he say where he was going?"

At this, the young man looked at them suspiciously. "Can I ask what this is regarding?"

"We're federal agents," Chloe said, thinking quickly. "We have some questions about a client and some potential illegal activity. We wanted to give Mr. Stephenson a heads-up. We have some questions about the client."

"Oh, okay," he said, suddenly interested and helpful again. "Do you have his cell number?"

"We do," Rhodes said. And they did; she had tried calling it twice on the way into Baltimore. "He isn't answering it."

"What sort of mood did he seem to be in when he left?" Chloe asked.

"I'm sorry, but I really didn't notice. Perhaps he went home for something? I can give you that address if you need it."

"Thanks, but we already have it," Rhodes said. She was already turning away, headed back for the door.

Chloe gave the young man a quick nod of thanks and then followed suit. As she hurried back to the car, she could not help but wonder if the call from the Central District officer had spooked Stephenson.

And after he had gotten spooked, maybe he felt as if he was working against the clock.

As they pulled out of the parking lot, a knot started to form in Chloe's stomach. What if, while they were chasing this man down, he was currently killing his fourth victim?

She focused on that thought as she sped through early afternoon traffic, following Rhodes's instructions as they drove toward Wade Stephenson's home.

CHAPTER TWENTY FOUR

Exactly two and a half miles away from Stephenson's home, Anderson called Chloe's phone. She was driving so fast that she had Rhodes answer the call for her, placing the call on speaker mode.

"I thought you might want to know that we got some more details on Wade Stephenson," Anderson said. "He doesn't have a record, though one of his former co-workers says that they are pretty sure he and his ex-wife sometimes got into physical confrontations. I've checked with the Maine State Police in Augusta and if there was such a confrontation, it was never called in or place on any record."

"Ex-wife," Rhodes said. "So he's divorced."

"Yes. The co-worker speculated on that, too. They think the reason for Stephenson's move was the divorce, though they split about eight months ago."

"They have any guesses as to why he moved back out to Baltimore?"

"No. I asked that very question, and they weren't sure."

"Okay. One more thing... can you find out if Stephenson has OnStar on his car? If not, the next thing to do is to get a cell phone trace."

"Yeah, I can do that. Give me about ten minutes or so. I take it he's on the run?"

"I wouldn't say that just yet," Chloe said. "But the call he got earlier from you guys seemed to scare him. His receptionist said he left work within fifteen minutes or so of when that call would have ended. We're headed to his home address right now."

"Let me know if you need anything else. I'll get back to you as soon as I know anything."

Rhodes killed the call as Chloe quickly approached the final turn in the directions that would lead them to Stephenson's house. Chloe was sitting rigid in her seat, scanning the side of the road for a mailbox with the correct address on the side. Rhodes was also sitting up expectantly, her hand reflexively ready to grab the door handle and open it. They were not quite at the point of rushing up and bursting into the home with guns drawn just yet but Chloe could feel it coming. Things were growing more and more tense, the sense of cat-and-mouse starting to overtake them, fueled by the fact that Wade Stephenson had left work immediately following the call from Anderson and the police.

Stephenson's neighborhood was nice in a generic sort of way. The houses sat fairly close to one another, little strips of lawn separating them and nothing more. His house looked very much like the ones that surrounded it, the only differences in them being the color of the siding and the structure and makeup of the porches.

Chloe pulled into Stephenson's driveway. The garage was closed and there were no other cars in the driveway. They rushed to the front door and Chloe wasted no time in knocking. She waited ten seconds and when there was no response of any kind, she knocked again, shouting this time as well.

"Mr. Stephenson, I need you to open up."

Rhodes gave her a simple hand gesture, ending it by pointing to the side lawn. *I'm going around to check the back,* this sign said. Chloe nodded and waited until Rhodes was around the side of the house before she tried knocking again.

"Mr. Stephenson, this is the FBI. If you are home, I need you to answer the door right away!"

Still, there was no answer. Impatient, Chloe ran off of the porch and to the garage. She ran along the side of it, hoping there might be a window that looked inside. There was no such window though, so there was no way for her to know for sure if Stephenson was home. She hurried back to the front door, snaking past it and to the single window that sat along the porch. She peered inside and though the blinds were drawn, she could make out a small dining room. It was tidy and, more importantly, empty.

As she stepped away from the window, Rhodes came running back around from the other side of the house. "There are two windows on the back porch," she said. "One looks into a kitchen and adjoined living room. The other looks into a small study. Both are empty. I don't think Stephenson is home."

That knot of worry drew tighter in Chloe's stomach. He had left work in a hurry and had *not* gone home. If he was indeed their killer, it seemed like a good bet that he was tracking up number four while they stood on his front porch like a couple of idiots.

When Chloe's phone rang, it scared them both badly. When she answered it, she did so quickly—so quickly that she did not notice the low battery indicator. "This is Fine," she said, doing her best to stomp down her worry.

"It's Anderson. Lo and behold, Wade Stephenson does indeed have OnStar in his car. A 2019 Honda Accord. I just spoke with a rep that was able to track it for me. I have an address, and it's less than fifteen minutes away from Stephenson's home. That's the good news."

"Is there bad news?"

"There is. He's at the home of a man named Thomas Robb. Robb was a linebacker for the Cougars during that championship year."

Chloe started dashing down the porch steps as she nearly screamed into the phone. "Send me that address now!"

With no siren bubble to place on the top of the car, Chloe ran her flashers and laid down on her horn during the trip to Thomas Robb's home. The fifteen-minute drive took less than seven minutes this way, as well as a ding to the back of the car when Chloe took a turn too fast and struck a street sign. But she barely even registered the event as it happened, her every muscle focused on getting to Robb's house ... hopefully in time to save his life.

Thomas Robb lived in a slightly better home than Wade Stephenson. It was a high-scale neighborhood with larger yards to go along with the larger and nicer houses. Again, this was yet another thing that Chloe barely noticed, because when they pulled into Robb's driveway, she spotted the 2019 Accord parked by a Yukon.

This time when Chloe and Rhodes got out both of their hands hovered over their sidearms. They flanked the porch, falling in step with one another like a well-oiled machine. Chloe knocked, but only because it was protocol. As far as she was concerned it was a waste of time. Their killer was still inside and if they were lucky, Thomas Robb might still be alive.

They waited five seconds and got no response. Chloe nodded to Rhodes and stepped aside. Rhodes was the stronger of the two—a fact she liked to remind Chloe of in jest here and there—and had no issues using that strength when it was needed.

She took a long stride backward, pivoted slightly, and sprang forward with a well-placed kick. The result was immediate. The door flew in, taking a good portion of the siding along the frame with it. One of the hinges clattered musically to the floor. As the door swung open, both women headed inside, Chloe taking out her Glock and taking the lead.

The house was eerily quiet, so quiet that Chloe thought she could still hear the clinking of the busted hinge echoing in its empty spaces. They crossed a small foyer and then the house split off into three directions: a big living space ahead, a hallway to the right, and the kitchen to the left. Chloe proceeded straight ahead into the living room while Rhodes opted for the hallway. They split off from one another, the silence of the house slowly becoming unnerving.

The living room was nicely kept, though it looked a bit like a frat house: sports magazines everywhere, framed sports memorabilia on the walls, and a bookcase crammed with old DVDs and books on sports, mixing drinks, and a few collections of nude photography. Chloe saw no signs of a struggle, no indication that anything violent had happened here.

As she neared the back of the living room and stepped foot into the kitchen, she started to her the murmuring of at least two voices. They were low but distinct, coming from somewhere else within the house. Chloe stood still, tracking where the voice were coming from. She scanned the area and saw a door at the far end of the kitchen, just where a small mudroom and laundry room served as the back of the house. The door was clearly a back door of some kind, complete with a large window that was covered in partially opened blinds. Sunlight poured through from outside, painting little light marks on the kitchen floor.

"Rhodes," she hissed. "Out back."

Rhodes appeared at the mouth of the hallway, entering the living room with footsteps so soft Chloe could not hear them at all. Rhodes spotted the back door and nodded toward it with an inquisitive stare. Chloe nodded and waited for Rhodes to fall in behind her.

Chloe walked to the door and cautiously parted two of the blinds wider. She could see someone moving around out there, but it was a slow movement. Whatever that motion was, it did not seemed to be a struggle of any kind. Now, closer to the door, she could hear one of the voices a bit clearer. It was a male voice, saying: "I can't believe you never told anyone else."

She was still uncertain if it was necessary to be carrying her Glock, so she slowly holstered it, just in case. Rhodes did not, though she lowered it out of sight as Chloe reached out and opened the door.

She swung it open quickly, the blinds making just enough noise to attract the attention of the two men sitting on the patio the door opened onto. One of the men was standing by the back railing, sipping on a drink; he froze mid-sip when he saw them. The other man was sitting in a lounge chair pressed against the far side of the patio.

"Who the f—" the man with the drink started, but then he saw Rhodes's gun, held down low but still just as threatening.

"We're with the FBI," Chloe said. She reached into her jacket pocket and withdrew her ID.

"Are you kidding me?" the second man said. He looked angry and terrified at the same time. At least thirty years had taken its toll on him, but the face Chloe saw was indeed a much older version of the Wade Stephenson she had seen in the yearbook.

"Mr. Stephenson, we need to speak with you," Chloe said.

"Fuck that," the first man—apparently Thomas Robb—said. "You just broke into my house! How did you even get in?"

"We will cover all of that momentarily," Chloe said, doing everything she could not to lose her patience. "For now, we need to speak with Mr. Robb."

"Look, I told the police I don't enjoy talking about that part of my life," Stephenson said.

"Understand that," Chloe said. "But they had good reason for calling. And we really need to speak with you. So we can either do it here or—"

"I said *no*! I'm not going to be a part of this."

Chloe nearly tried once again. But as she took a step forward, she noticed something that momentarily froze her in place. Wade Stephenson was sitting back in the lounge chair, leaning back a bit to make sure they could see that he had no intention of going anywhere with them. In doing so, the bottom of his pants were pulled tight, revealing his socks.

Black athletic socks.

Chloe slowly unholstered his sidearm again. She did not point it at Stephenson but she made quite the display of getting it out. "Mr. Stephenson, I need you to come with us. I am no longer asking."

Stephenson looked terrified now, sitting up and looking over at Robb. Robb looked scared, too, but there was also disgust on his face. "You can't just bust in someone's house and do this," Robb said.

"This is outrageous!" Stephenson said. He had jumped to his feet, but stood his ground. His gaze was now darting back and forth between the gun and both of the agents who had caught up to him.

"Do you know why we're here, Mr. Stephenson?" Rhodes asked.

"Of course I do! You've hunted me down because I was rude to the police officer that wanted to quiz me on some of the worst moments of my life."

"That's only part of the issue," Chloe said.

He was close to crying now, his face starting to turn red as the corners of his eyes started to get moist. "I haven't done anything…"

"Good. But we have to take you in."

As if sensing where Chloe was taking the situation, Rhodes pivoted around her and withdrew her handcuffs.

"Oh, come on now," Robb bellowed. "Is that really necessary?"

"No, I'll go already!" Stephenson said. Chloe could tell he wanted to scream at them, but was afraid it might turn into weeping. "Shit! Just… give me some space."

Rhodes took a step back and allowed Stephenson to walk forward, toward the back door. Chloe fell in behind him so that they were flanking him, one ahead and one behind.

"What can I do?" Robb called out to Stephenson.

"Nothing," Stephenson said without turning. There was anger in his voice now, and he sounded absolutely livid when he said: "Nothing at all. By the time my lawyer is through with them after this insanity, it'll be *them* that needs the help."

Chloe wasn't worried. In fact, all she could think about were the black athletic socks on Stephenson's feet and how he had retreated from work upon getting a phone call from the police. Sure, there were some doubts to be ironed out, but as far as Chloe was concerned, Wade Stephenson was a very likely suspect.

CHAPTER TWENTY FIVE

Danielle opened her eyes and for a moment, she was frozen in the grip of something very much like a panic attack. She was sitting on the ground, and she had no idea where she was. But then the empty shape of the old slaughterhouse started to sink in and her memories took it.

She'd had to walk away... had to get some sleep. But she hadn't wanted to do it in front of her father. Just a nap, that's all she'd asked for. But it had been nearly dawn when she'd made that decision and now the sunlight filtering in through the cracks of the warehouse told her that it was much later than that. Scrambling to her feet, she checked her watch and saw that it was almost noon.

Something croaked from behind her. She nearly screamed in fright but then realized it was only her father. She shook the sleep out of her head and walked back across the large empty central area, back to the room where she had strung him up. He looked at her with a perfect blend of fear and desperation as she entered the room.

"Danielle... I can't feel my arms."

"Good."

She walked to her bag and took out the water for him. She walked over to him and he was opening his mouth for it before he she even reached him. He sucked it down greedily and opened his mouth again when she offered him a cracker. She then gave him two more. She was going to have to kill him soon. Sure, that would be brutal... but what she was doing now was akin to torture. And while she firmly believed that he deserved it, she just didn't have the stomach for it.

When he was done with the last cracker, Danielle turned away from him and walked quickly back out into the large central room she had been napping in. She started crying as she made her way across the room and to the large exit doors. She was fully crying by the time she got outside, the hot Texas sun beaming down on her. She made her way to her car, carefully backed out of her hiding spot along the edge of the forest, and headed back out toward the tiny town of Millseed.

The drive into town was a blur of tears and screaming. What the hell was she doing? What had she become? What sort of a monster had her father turned her into?

Somehow, through tears and the spooky will of memory, Danielle managed to find her way to Millseed's one single convenience store. She parked at the far edge, hoping against hope that Millseed's sorry excuse for town maintenance had not yet gotten overzealous enough to remove the pay phone from the edge of the lot.

As she neared the edge, she saw it standing like a relic from a much older time. She had used it several times during her time here, usually when she was unable to pay for her cell service. That had been a little over four years ago. The thing had sounded terrible back then—so she knew it was a gamble to hope it worked now. She dug a handful of quarters out of the ashtray compartment she always tossed loose change into, feeling a little silly.

Still, she marched to the pay phone with purpose. When she picked the receiver up out of the cradle, her heart stilled in her chest when she did not hear a dial tone. But then she remembered nothing would happen until the money was dropped in. She used $1.75 to place the call to Chloe's number.

There was a series of clicks, what sounded like an odd pulse of sorts, and then a single ring. Following the ring, there was another click and then her sister's recorder voice.

"No," Danielle whined. She nearly hung up right then and there but took into account Chloe's work. It was actually unrealistic to expect Chloe to answer the phone.

Only, I know my sister, she thought. *She's probably worried out of her mind. She'd answer the phone if she thought it was me… right?*

Chloe's voice told her to leave a message after the beep. Danielle did so, unable to stop the stream of words that came out.

"Chloe… I've done something stupid and I don't know… I don't know what to do. I'm in some trouble, Chloe. I'm in Millseed, Texas. Dad is with me and I…"

She stopped here, better sense coming to the forefront. Her sister worked with the FBI. Admitting why she had her father here would cause a shitstorm—not just for her, but for Chloe as well. So she ended it simply, trying her best to hide the emotion in her voice.

"Just… come out here when you can, please. A big empty concrete building on State Road 14. I'm sorry…"

With that, she hung up. She went back to her car and sat in it for a very long time, staring at the pay phone. When she felt that she had enough courage to head back to the slaughterhouse and finally make a decision—to either kill her father or free him—she started the engine and headed back to face him.

She parked in the same spot, amazed at how easy it was. Yes, this town was in the middle of nowhere, but still… she felt totally isolated as she walked the overgrown field between the edge of the forest and the cracked back lot of the old slaughterhouse. Her watch read 12:57 when she crossed the large open area where so many pigs and cows had been butchered. Danielle looked idly to the faint stains on the floor as she headed back to see her dad. She still had no idea what she was going to do. But she knew she needed to make the decision now. She had to—

She stopped in the doorway, looking into the room.

The ropes she had used to tie her father into that uncomfortable position were dangling uselessly from the tracks above.

But there was no sign of Aiden Fine.

"What the hell…"

The only way out of the room was the glassless window to the right, but it was about eight feet off the ground. She could not imagine any scenario in which her father would have been able to scramble out of it. So, of course, he likely just went running out through the main slaughtering area—the same space she had just come across.

She turned to check outside, thinking he possibly left some trace of where he escaped to. Panic and fear started to rise up in her as she started forward.

She took only three steps before something hard hit her in the back of the head. She let out a cry as her knees buckled. She was barely able to catch herself with her hands before her head slammed into the concrete floor.

She tried to turn over to see what had happened. She saw her father for just a moment, standing over her with a large chunk of wood—some old board from the back of the building where she had seen a few scraps of it piled up. He raised it again to strike her one more time but before she could even see it fall, the world dimmed quickly, fading out to nothing but a stark black that felt very much like sleep.

CHAPTER TWENTY SIX

Stephenson had been absolutely outraged that he'd been forced to ride to the station in the backseat of Chloe and Rhodes's car. Every mile they put behind them, Stephenson seemed to get more and more irritated, which made him a bit more courageous. When Chloe or Rhodes would ask him a question he would only glare at them, sometimes with his arms folded like a pouting child. Chloe and Rhodes were fine with it for the time being. Chloe, in particular, did not mind allowing the suspect to feel as if they had some power in the situation while they were en route, because she knew that once they got into an interrogation room, that was her turf. And no matter what kind of threats or pleas Stephenson might make, he would ultimately be under her thumb.

He did try one more power play when they had him in the interrogation room, though. Both Chloe and Rhodes remained on their feet, Chloe feeling the case nearing its end and unable to sit down.

"Mr. Stephenson, I'd like to know why—"

"I'm not answering anything until I talk to my lawyer."

"Under normal circumstances, I'd allow that. But there are pressing things at stake here and—"

"*Allow* it?" Stephenson barked. "That's my *right*."

"A right I'm choosing to quash for now," Chloe said. "Mr. Stephenson, if you had allowed the officer you spoke with earlier to finish, you might have recognized that there was a very good reason for him to call you."

Stephenson said nothing. He even cracked a little grin at her to show her he meant what he'd said: not a single word until his lawyer was present.

"It seems that many of the boys who bullied you in high school grew up to be men that someone had something against. Three of them are now dead, Mr. Stephenson. Murdered, and all within just a few days."

She watched his face to see any signs of shock or surprise. But as it was, his face was already such a strange mixture of emotion that it was hard to tell.

"Are you serious?" he finally asked.

"Yes. Bo Luntz, Richard Wells, and Gordon Nettles."

"Mr. Stephenson, you tried out to be kicker, right?" Rhodes asked.

He nodded dimly, his mind still digesting the names that he'd just heard. "They're all dead?"

"Yes," Chloe said. "Earlier today, we ran through most of the names in the yearbook from the championship year to see if we could find any other potential victims, *or* a killer."

"You think ... hold on. You think *I'm* the killer?"

"Based on the facts as we know them as well as your history with the deceased, yes ... we have reason to suspect you."

He let out a high-pitched laugh, one that made both Chloe and Rhodes jump. "That's ... no. That's absolutely insane."

"Why did you leave work after receiving the call from the police?" Chloe asked.

"Because it ruined my entire day. I hate to pull the victim card here, trust me ... but the things those assholes did to me back then ... I never got over it. I told very few people about it and somehow, here I am anyway, having to face it all over again."

"Then why come back to the Baltimore area?" Rhodes asked. "What was wrong with Maine?"

"My soon to be ex-wife is what is wrong with Maine. And I also got a good job offer here. I would have been a fool to pass it up."

"I saw that; your name is already part of the firm."

"Yes. It stands to be a very rewarding job."

"Okay, so tell me this, then," Chloe said, unimpressed with his career ambitions. "When you left work, you went to the home of Thomas Robb…another person who played on that championship Cougars team. You can understand how that would fit the behavior of the killer, correct?"

A brief look of understanding flashed across his face, but only for a moment. He nodded but then, almost comically, started shaking his head. "Thomas and I connected on Facebook. He invited me over for a few beers when I moved back into town. We ended up talking about those days…back in high school. And the bullying came up…"

"Did Thomas Robb ever bully you?" Rhodes asked.

"No. He never did the bullying, though he was usually around. Watching, like so many others."

"What was done to you?" Chloe asked. "We've spoken to another bullying victim who gave some graphic details. So if certain things *were* done to you, well…we don't expect you to tell us all of them. But can you confirm that you were in some way, shape, or form attacked and bullied by one of the three men I have just named?"

Stephenson only nodded. His eyes looked distant as he peered into the past, staring down traumas he had been unable to put behind him.

"Here's where we are currently," Chloe said. "I'm going to give you three dates and expanses of time. If you can account for your whereabouts—and if there are witnesses to corroborate your details—then we can start working towards getting you out of here."

"I can certainly try." But he sounded defeated—like he knew there was no way he was going to be able to give them what they wanted. His eyes found the table and his expression became very downcast.

"Let's start with—"

But again, he cut her off. And this time, there was none of that anger and rage. He knew he was in trouble and, Chloe thought, was starting to accept it.

"No. No more until my lawyer gets here."

Oddly enough, his somber tones were more powerful than his angry ones. Chloe and Rhodes simply looked at one another, feeling precious time slipping by, as they waited for Stephenson's lawyer to arrive.

While Chloe and Rhodes waited for Stephenson's lawyer, Detective Anderson and a few other officers went out to Stephenson's home. Another had also ventured out to Thomas Robb's residence to ask what they had been speaking about and if there had ever been any ill will between them in the past.

It did not take long before Anderson was calling with some very interesting findings. It was Rhodes's phone that rang this time, breaking them out of a silence in their makeshift office as they stared at the whiteboard where they had tried inserting Stephenson into the equation in order to come up with a winner.

Rhodes answered and put the call on speaker, placing it in the center of the table. "Okay, we're both here," Rhodes said.

"Good to know," Anderson said. "Fine's phone went straight to voicemail."

Chloe reached into her pocket and checked her phone. She rolled her eyes when she found it dead. "Sorry. Sleeping in a holding cell last night, I wasn't really afforded the opportunity to charge my phone. I guess I just never even thought about it today."

"No worries. Listen, I'm standing in Stephenson's bedroom right now. The top drawer of his bureau is loaded down with black athletic socks."

"In pairs?" Chloe asked.

Anderson chuckled at the absurdity of the question but then seemed to understand what she was looking for. "No. It's just a big pile of single socks."

"You mind bagging up a few and bringing them in?" Chloe asked. "If those are a match for the ones pulled out of the throats of the victims…"

"Already ahead of you."

"Any word from the officer that went out to speak with Robb?"

"Not yet. I'll let you know if there's anything worth telling."

"Thanks," Rhodes said, ending the call. She and Chloe looked at one another across the table, weighing it all out.

"Everything lines up," Rhodes said. "He was at the home of an old player. He's small statured like the coroner thinks the killer would be. He just happened to move back into town about a week before the murders started..."

"But he said he and Robb had hung out at least once before," Chloe pointed out.

"So maybe he was trying to get a layout of the house. Remember...this killer knew how to get into the homes without tripping alarms."

Chloe considered this for a moment. She did indeed feel as if they currently had the killer in custody. So why was there a nagging doubt in the back of her mind? Why did she feel as if they had missed something quite important?

Maybe it's not this case, she thought. *Maybe my mind is still hung up on Danielle. And how long has my phone been dead? An hour? Two? What if she tried to call me in that time?*

She felt the shape of her phone in her pocket, feeling the need to get it charged as soon as possible. But she then looked at the whiteboard, to the scattered files on the table in front of her. Everything Rhodes had said was true: Stephenson fit the size suggested by the coroner, he had just moved back into town before the murders started, he had the black socks, he had the motive, he had been at Robb's house...

All the pieces fit. The fact that he was now nervously waiting for his lawyer before saying anything else put them all together. Although she found it hard to believe, it seemed their killer was currently sitting in an interrogation room less than twenty feet away.

Case closed.

Now, of course, there was Danielle to worry about. And she doubted that particular problem would be wrapped up so neatly.

CHAPTER TWENTY SEVEN

Danielle opened her eyes and let out a scream right away. Only, she could not hear the scream. It was muffled and quiet, though it did rattle her head—a head that felt as if it had been cracked right in half.

She felt something tight around her mouth, pushing against her face. She was staring up into a dingy brown ceiling. Old beehives and bird's nests were crammed in between some of the rafters and posts.

The slaughterhouse...

She tried sitting up, only to realize that she was already sitting. Her neck had been craned back, forcing her to look up at the ceiling. Yes, she was already seated, sitting in a chair that felt very rickety and thin beneath her. She tried standing but could not. She felt ropes around her wrists, tied behind her back. Her legs were also tied to the thin spindly legs of the chair.

She screamed again. This time when the scream was blocked, she realized that she was gagged. Her head reeled, making her cry out in pain as well as shock and alarm. She looked around quickly, her eyes finally realizing that the evening had grown dark. The inside of the slaughterhouse looked gloomy now, not bright and shadow-filled as it had been when she had come back from calling Choe.

And what happened then? What did I come back to?

Her father...

She moaned against the gag as she remembered him standing over her with the board.

"It's okay, Danielle."

The voice came from behind her. It was her father's voice and he sounded ... well, he sounded *happy*.

He stepped into view, smiling thinly at her. He held her bag in his right hand. It was unzipped and she saw the gleam of the small pistol. She moaned against the gag, hating herself for how sad and defeated it sounded.

"You really did mean to kill me, didn't you?" Aiden asked. "That's a pretty dainty little gun you're packing, but it would have done the job for sure."

He tossed the bag down and flexed his right arm. He looked tired and slightly deranged. If Danielle had not trusted him before, she was downright terrified of him now.

"I'm sorry I hit you," he said. "Even after everything you did to me, I did not want to hit you. I hope you understand that. I was afraid I'd accidentally killed you there for a minute or so. I'd never purposefully hurt you, Danielle ... but you didn't leave me much of a choice, now did you? See ... I think you and I need to have a talk. I'd love to think I could take that gag off but ... no, I don't think I'll take that chance."

He was observing her in the same way a small child might look at a bug it had never seen before. Despite the things he was saying about not hurting her, that look made her not believe him.

"It's become clear to me that nothing will be good enough for you. Danielle, I did my time for the crimes I committed. I paid my penance. But you ... you're never going to let it go, are you? And from what I can tell, you've got Chloe thinking along those same lines now, too. You know ... after your mother died, I wasn't close to either of you, but Chloe ... at least she made an effort, you know?"

She wanted to scream at him, wanted to tell him that he was never worth the effort. They knew everything about him now and she would never forgive him. As far as she was concerned, he should still be in prison with nothing to look forward to but his death.

"I suppose I always knew things would never be the same ... that neither of you would fully trust me. But then ... well, something happened, I suppose. Chloe started digging and the two of you uncovered my little secret about Ruthanne."

She sensed where this was going and prayed he had not discovered the recorder. She'd left it out, away from the bag. It was still sitting on her little throne of pallets, tucked under one of the boards. She tried not to look hopeful, though—not a difficult task, considering how angry and afraid she was feeling in that moment.

He hesitated here, the expression on his face one of concern. To Danielle, it seemed as if he was wrestling with himself, trying to come to terms with something.

"I just...after all this time, it's hard to say it...to face it. But you've been right all along, Danielle. I know Chloe was the more level-headed of you, has that drive and determination about her. But you...you always had this gut instinct thing, even from the age of five or so. And you were right. As if that damned diary didn't already paint the picture well enough—yes, I did it. I killed her. Ruthanne was going to try to take the blame...that's how that all got mixed up and confusing. She knew about it, of course. And she had no issue with it. I suppose, really, it was her idea. She motivated me to do it. But in the end, I did it."

Got you, you son of a bitch...

The thought swept through her mind like a hurricane.

But if he had found her recorder...if he had found it and turned it off, then this meant nothing. It was his word against hers.

"Now, even saying that, you have to know that it was an accident. I mean, I probably would have before it was said and done, but when it happened...it truly was an accident. I just lost control and, as you know, she went falling down those stairs.

"Now...there. You have it straight from my mouth. I hope you can forgive me, Danielle. I really do. I know how my mistakes affected your life and I am truly sorry for that."

Danielle had no idea where it came from, but she felt tears streaming down her face. Oddly enough, it was the presence of those tears, feeling them warm and coursing down her cheeks, that caused her to break. She let out a moan of sorrow that sounded like some pained and dying animal from behind the gag.

When she saw that he was starting to cry, too, she looked away and screamed. She screamed until her throat hurt. She rocked in the chair, desperate to get out, to get away from him. She wasn't even sure if she could hurt him now. She just had to get away…where her eyes did not have to take in the sight of him.

She rocked and screamed. The chair creaked under her weight and, beyond all of that, there was something else. She sensed it—she *felt* it—but she did her best to not let him see it.

As she rocked in the chair, letting out so many years of pain and frustration, Danielle felt the knot in the rope that was holding her hands together behind her back start to come loose.

CHAPTER TWENTY EIGHT

As it turned out, there were no alibis at all for Wade Stephenson. Even after his lawyer arrived and they spent forty-five minutes conferring, the best they could come up with was allowing the police to search Stephenson's internet history to prove that he had been home on the afternoon of the murder of Richard Wells. To make things worse for Stephenson, he admitted that interviewing co-workers would only lead to further speculation of his guilt because he had been leaving early almost every day since he started the job. After all, one of the perks of taking the job was keeping his own hours; he had been arriving to work very early so he could leave a few hours early.

"I know the socks are all we really have to go on at the moment," Rhodes said, "but it really looks like he's the guy."

Chloe, Rhodes, and Anderson were huddled around the desk in the whiteboard office, trying to make sense of it all. Anderson had spoken with Stephenson and his lawyer while Chloe and Rhodes had been briefed on the conversation the local officers had had with Thomas Robb. Nothing had come out of that conversation other than Robb's disdain for how the FBI and the local police had handled the situation. And he was still plenty pissed off about his front door.

"Robb said Stephenson had been over twice before," Chloe said. "And the first time, they mostly talked about high school. Ended up bonding over it, right? Robb apologized for never saying anything to try to stop the bullying."

"Sounds about right, verbatim," Anderson said.

"I'd love to think things work out so cleanly so many years later," Chloe said, "but am I the only one that's not buying it?"

"It seems very Hallmark-like for sure," Rhodes said. "But everything else lines up."

"Well, except for the fact that Robb says there was never a moment where he felt as if he were in danger," Chloe said. "And that he invited Stephenson over."

Neither Rhodes nor Anderson said anything to this. Chloe knew that on paper it did appear as if Stephenson was at the very least a highly likely suspect in the case. But something felt off and she was not able to let it go. She tried to remind herself that she was still hung up on the entire Danielle case but that only served to remind her that her sister was still out there somewhere, missing and maybe even in danger.

Are you sure that's what it is? she asked herself. *Can't just assume here; this killer acts fast and if we're wrong about Stephenson, the killer could already be out there planning the next death.*

She had felt that cross-referencing people in the yearbook had been working, though it was monotonous. But they still didn't have time for the redundancy of it all: leaving messages, finding the occasional disconnected number. There was just no time. She had to get back there and question him, to be sure. She wasn't sure she'd be able to deal with the regret of it later if…

Regrets…

Suddenly, almost like a lightning bolt passing through her head, she thought of Coach Dick Yancy. He had mentioned having regrets but it had been in an almost dreamlike way—a way that had, at the time, made her think he was nothing more than an old man looking back on a life he wished he had lived differently.

And he had also been able to recall certain stats and facts about that championship team … but not player names. She had passed it off before, not thinking anything of it because of his age. But how could he remember stats, facts, and small details like that but not the names of players?

It made her think he might be hiding something.

He'd also admitted to some of his players behaving inappropriately at times—sometimes bad enough to be pointed out by the school, though no appropriate punishments were ever doled out except for the quarterback being kicked off the team.

It made her wonder what, exactly, his regrets were centered around ... and if they might be related to the Summit Hills Cougars. And if there were regrets, there were almost certainly some dark secrets shadowing them.

They were able to get past the receptionist at Everwood Retirement Village rather easily, but the nurse on duty was another matter entirely. She halted Chloe and Rhodes as they walked through the common room and toward the hall Yancy resided in.

"Mr. Yancy is not doing well at all," she said. She was a stout woman who reminded Chloe of one of her sixth-grade teachers— an unpleasant woman who, while quite pretty, seemed to contain the wrath of Hell in her scowl alone. "In fact, he has seemed rather distressed and very confused since your last visit."

"I apologize for that," Chloe said. "And while I can't give you certain details of why we need to speak with him, I *can* tell you this: as of right now, he is the only meaningful link that we have between three recently murdered men."

"I don't doubt your need to meet with him, but I can't under good judgment allow—"

"Three men have been killed in six days," Rhodes said. "This killer is fast and we have no idea how many more there might be. But Mr. Yancy might."

"You can be there in the room with us," Chloe said. "But this is very urgent. And at the risk of sounding like a total bitch, I can make a few calls that will *make* you have to let us speak with him. Please ... let's do this the easy way."

The nurse scowled at them again and then let out a sigh that might have been able to shake the side of a building. "I'll give you ten minutes," she said finally. "And if I think he's getting worse because of your presence, the meeting is over. You can go back and make all the calls you want, but I have a job to do—just the same as you."

"Thank you," Chloe said, though the nurse was already storming off down the hallway.

She did not stop at Yancy's room, though. She led them to the end of the hallway and opened a set of double doors that led out to a small but quite well-maintained flower garden. There were a few residents sitting on benches, one of whom was giggling in a child-like way as a butterfly perched on his leg.

Yancy was sitting on the right side of the garden. He was alone on a bench positioned by a small concrete fountain. He looked up as the nurse led Chloe and Rhodes to him. He seemed alarmed to see them again at first but then he smirked. It almost seemed as if he had nearly been expecting them to show up again.

"Agents," he said. "Couldn't get enough, eh?"

"Something like that," Chloe said. "Mr. Yancy, can we sit down?"

He nodded and scooted over. It was clear that there would only be enough room for one of them, so Rhodes stayed on her feet.

"Mr. Yancy," the nurse said, "if this gets irritating to you or if you want them to leave at any point, you just let me know."

Yancy waved the comment away. "It's fine. I thought they'd come back."

"And why is that?" Rhodes asked.

"Our conversation…it didn't quite seem finished, did it?"

"No, it did not," Chloe said. "And in the interest of saving time, I'd like to remind you about something you told me. Something about having regrets. I need you to be as honest as you can and please tell me if any of those regrets came from the time you spent coaching that championship team with Wells, Nettles, and Luntz."

He let out a sigh that nearly matched the one the nurse had let out moments ago. He nodded almost right away, though. "Yeah. And I'm sorry I didn't say anything before. But I've sat on this for so damned long. I was pushing middle age when it happened, you know…that championship team. And I just…I kept ignoring it until it became this thing in the back of my head that I had almost convinced myself never happened…so I could die without admitting to it."

"What was it?" Chloe asked. "Mr. Yancy, if you did something wrong, given your age and condition, we could—"

"No, it wasn't me. It was something I knew about and never did anything about…"

"Was it one of your players?"

Yancy nodded. He looked at the nurse and then at the flowers beside him—a few withering roses, mostly.

"I haven't told anyone about this since it happened. Back then, I only told a single person…and that was the superintendent of the school district. But they covered it up pretty quickly, as I knew they would. Which is why I took it to them." He gathered his thoughts for a moment, and started trembling.

"Mr. Yancy," the nurse said. "Do you need—"

"Let me do this," he snapped. "Let me finally get this out. Agents…you were right. Some of those boys were nothing but trouble. But as a coach, I just looked at their talent, you know? I let them get away with some things here and there…bullying kids in the locker room during gym class, mooning people, drinking beers at lunchtime, that sort of thing. It was stupid, but that's in the past and I can't change that. But there was one other thing…one thing that made me wonder if I had…I don't know…enabled them."

He stopped here, and the nurse stepped forward. But Yancy shook his head. "Sit down. I've started, and I'm going to get it out. I have to…if I want to die peacefully, I have to."

"Mr. Yancy, it's okay," Chloe said as softly as she could.

"I hate that I don't remember the poor girl's name," he said randomly. She was a cheerleader…came to me one evening when I was at school late, going over a game plan for the week's game. Any other day, she would have gone to the cheerleading coach, but she had already left for the day. She comes into my office, and she's crying. She's sort of zoned out, you know, like she's trying to process something. I saw the bruise on her face right away but ... I didn't see the way she was walking until she left ..."

"Did they beat her?" Chloe asked.

Yancy nodded, but the pain in his eyes indicated he wasn't done. "She said there were five of them. One of them grabbed her as she was heading out to the parking lot and yanked her into the downstairs entrance to the boys' locker room. Later, when it was all done, she said they only hit her once, right in the face. Made her dizzy. But ... they ..."

He was crying now and although it was obvious the nurse wanted to put a stop to it, she, too, understood that something monumental was happening. Not only was this old man unburdening his heart after over thirty years of torture, he was giving Chloe and Rhodes exactly what they had been looking for.

"One of them opened one of the equipment lockers and pushed her in ... but just from her upper back up. The rest was still sticking out. One of the boys pushed against the door, squeezing her between the frame and the door so she couldn't move. She was wearing her cheerleading outfit, so I guess it was easy for them to ... to undress her like that. And they took turns. One after the other ..."

He was hitching now, fighting for breath. Chloe had gotten enough to be satisfied. She could not put him through anything else. She had a name and a confession ... but Yancy was still going.

"I was mad at first, wanted to hang those boys by their nuts in front of the school. Especially when I went to see if they were still there. But all there was ... on the floor ... blood and their stuff ... they had tried to clean it up, but ..."

"Mr. Yancy, that's enough," Chloe said.

"I went to the superintendent because I knew there it's where it would end up anyway. And in about two days, it was all covered up. That fucking championship blinded us all. Someone on the board paid off the family. Not much money, either ..."

His words were growing lazy, as if he were getting very tired. Chloe and Rhodes looked to the nurse and saw that she was crying. The nurse gave them both a curt little nod toward the double doors that would lead them back inside. Chloe started first, and Rhodes quickly fell in behind her.

As the doors slowly shut behind them, Chloe could hear Yancy, still sniffling as he drew his big, shaky breaths. It made Chloe feel slightly sick to the stomach.

"I know we have a killer to catch," Rhodes said, "but if these recently murdered men were among the five that did that... I'm glad they're dead."

Chloe felt similarly but did not say as much. Instead, she was fixated on the fact that the girl Yancy mentioned had been a cheerleader. It reminded her of another woman they had met recently who had also been a cheerleader.

She pulled out her phone to call Angie Wells but decided not to. There was no way Angie had been a cheerleader and not shared the story with her.

That is, of course, unless the cheerleader in Yancy's story had *been* Angie Wells.

CHAPTER TWENTY NINE

They arrived at the Hilton Garden Inn twenty minutes later. Chloe was acting on nothing but a hunch, assuming that Angie would be staying overnight in Baltimore rather than leaving straight from Richard's funeral and flying back to Rhode Island. A quick check with the check-in desk confirmed that her gut was right. After checking Chloe's badge and ID, the woman behind the desk gave them Angie's room number. But as they rushed for the elevators, Chloe thought of Angie's mood when she'd last seen her in this same building. They'd been in the bar and Angie, while trying her best to seem unaffected by her ex-husband's death, had been trying to drown something with an endless supply of drinks.

"Hold on," Chloe said. "Let me check something..."

She veered away from the elevators and headed to the rear of the lobby, where the entrance to the bar area was dimly lit. Soft rock wafted out, as the place had not yet picked up for the night crowd. Because it was so slow—being only 6:47 in the evening—it was easy to spot the lone woman sitting at the left end of the bar. Thought the bar was dim, the lights behind it, shining through assorted liquor glasses, shone on Angie Wells's face.

Chloe approached the woman apprehensively, unsure of how much of an emotional toil the day had placed on her. So far, Angie had been hesitantly helpful; now, though, when she spotted Chloe, she rolled her eyes and shook her head. Chloe sat down next to her, Rhodes taking the stool beside her.

"Haven't I helped you enough?" Angie asked.

"You have," Chloe said. "You've been a tremendous help. However, we learned something today...something new. And I really need you to clear something up for me."

Angie sipped from her drink—a bright-colored martini of some kind—and looked to the bottles in front of her, as if already selecting her next drink.

"If I ask you to get out of here and leave me alone, what happens?" Angie asked.

"Typically, we'd have to leave and then go back to report it. We'd then file a report, get a warrant, and you'd be questioned anyway—with added suspicion due to your unwillingness to talk."

"Is this instance not typical?" Angie asked.

"I'm afraid not. Now, based on the new information we have, we'd be within our rights to arrest you if you were resistant."

Angie's look of confusion was genuine, but Chloe tried not to let it affect her. "Arrest me for what?"

"Either purposefully lying to me earlier or due to our suspicion of you potentially killing three men over the course of the past week."

"I did not lie to you," she said matter-of-factly.

"Did you perhaps fail to mention something, then? Maybe something pretty sick and twisted that you had tried to forget?"

Chloe felt a sense of urgency rush through her after saying this. She sensed that whatever Angie Wells said next would either nail her to the wall or prove her innocence. Chloe remained calm, though the bottles on the other side of the bar seemed very appealing in that moment.

"I take it you *have*?"

"Yes, I have. And I believe it happened to one of your fellow cheerleaders on that same championship year we've been talking about."

The color seemed to drain right out of Angie's face. Chloe wasn't quite ready to say it was a sign of guilt, but it *was* a sign of someone being confronted with something they had not been expecting.

"I don't know what you're talking about."

"You sure about that? Not some messed up piece of gossip about yourself or some other girl?"

"Why are you doing this?" It was an accusatory question, not one of general wonderment.

"Men are dead. Three. We expect more."

"Good."

The word was out before Angie could stop it. She even bit her lip when she understood what she had said and what it might mean.

Chloe braced herself, ready to go for her cuffs. "And what is that supposed to mean?"

Angie sighed and then shrugged. "I just... how did you find out?" Her voice was little more than a whisper. She downed the rest of the martini she had been working on and then looked toward the bartender, almost pleading.

"I can't tell you that. But it was someone on the inside."

"Someone at the school, I'd guess," Angie said. "None of the men would admit to it, I'm sure. And not too many of the other cheerleaders knew about it."

"But you did?" Rhodes asked.

"Yes. She told me and one other... but it was a few weeks afterwards. Her family got paid off. She..."

"What's her name?" Chloe asked.

Angie frowned and then looked to the bartender once more. When he caught her eye, she pointed to her glass and he nodded. Chloe wondered how many more she'd have after coming clean with whatever she was staring to unload.

"Claire Underhill. Nice girl. Very polite and petite and... pretty but not very popular, you know? Kept to herself most of the time."

"You were friends with her?"

"Not really. We only knew one another because we were both cheerleaders. But outside of practice and games, no... we never really hung out."

"What did she say to you when she told you what had happened?"

"Well, there were a few of us after a game one night, hanging behind the bleachers. We were drinking Boone's Farm and

161

chatting. And she just dropped it on us out of the blue. Said she was gang raped by five guys on the football team. She was drunk when she told us—I guess maybe that's *why* she told us. But she then said there were these people from the county school board that came by her house. She wasn't allowed to be part of the meeting, but they paid her parents to be quiet. And Claire...her family was always sort of poor...so I guess they took it."

"Any idea how much?" Rhodes asked.

"She wouldn't say. And we wouldn't really ask, you know. After that night, Claire never talked to us again. She quit the squad and after graduation, she became a ghost."

"Any idea where she might be living?" Chloe asked.

"Jersey, last I heard."

The bartender came over with a new martini and she started on it right away.

"Have you spoken to her?"

"No. I'm speculating. Things I've seen on Facebook, some phone conversations with old friends from high school...that sort of thing."

"Angie...do you know which players did this to her?"

Angie Wells looked like she might throw a punch any minute. She held on to her martini glass, perhaps to make sure she didn't start swinging. "I know what you want to ask me," she said. There was anger in her voice, but it was quelled. She was keeping it in check. It made Chloe wonder if she had been keeping that anger in check for years—ever since the day she had married Richard Wells.

"Then don't make me," Chloe said.

"The whole incident came up when we were dating. I wasn't sure he was actually one of them, but then I started wondering. There was one time when we were married—the first year, I think—when I waited for him to get shit-faced drunk and asked him. He didn't admit to it, but he broke down crying. Like, messy, gut-wrenching sobs. He didn't talk to me for about a week after that. So I stopped asking. I hate myself for it a bit but...I was married and I loved him. And the past is the past."

"Do you know if Bo Luntz and Gordon Nettles were involved?"

"According to Richard, Bo was certainly one of them. He never actually came out and gave that name, but the night I confronted him while drunk, he all but said Bo Luntz was one of them. And if Luntz was involved, I can damn near guarantee you Gordon Nettles was right there with him."

Chloe got to her feet and looked at Angie with as much sorrow as she could muster. She did feel sorry for the woman. More than that, she felt awful for forcing her to sit through these memories on the same day she had buried her husband.

"Agent Fine…you understand why I didn't tell you earlier, right?"

"I think so. You didn't want to remember him like that… *if* he did it."

"I think he did," she said. The comment was bold and unexpected. But the look on Angie's face was resigned. "I hate to say it and have never admitted it to myself until right now, but I think he did."

"Thank you, Mrs. Wells."

Angie didn't even give a nod of thanks as she turned away and gave the martini her full attention. Chloe and Rhodes walked away, both feeling solemn and somehow in mourning themselves, as they stalked back through the gloom of the bar. By the time they had reached the doors leading to the parking lot, Chloe had Anderson on the phone once again.

"I need all attention focused on hunting down a woman named Claire Underhill," she told him. "Current residence is likely in New Jersey, but I feel like she's been spending the last week or so in Baltimore. Looks like she might be our killer."

"I can absolutely do that, but I do have one thing for you … maybe nothing, but … I don't know."

"What's that?"

"We've been trying to call Thomas Robb, wanting to talk to him more about his knowledge of Wade Stephenson. He's been stand-offish up until now, but he's not answering his phone now. I'm to the point of wondering if I should send some guys over to check."

"You stick with the Claire Underhill lead," Chloe said. "Rhodes and I are about fifteen minutes from Robb's house. We'll swing by there."

"He could just be ignoring our calls. But…"

"No, it's a good idea to check it out, all things considered."

She ended the call and as she pocketed it, she put some speed in her step. Rhodes met her pace as they neared the car.

"What's wrong with Thomas Robb?" she asked.

"He's not answering his phone," Chloe said. And as she spoke the words, the certainty of the moment settled in. That sense of urgency flared up inside of her again. Even before she got behind the wheel, she felt all but certain that they would get to Thomas Robb's house and he would be dead.

"We better get going then," Rhodes said. "If you recall, I kicked that door down and made it quite easy for someone to break in."

Chapter Thirty

Thomas Robb was sitting on his back porch again, still rattled by the sudden appearance of the FBI agents earlier in the day. For one stark moment, he had feared they were there for him. It was ridiculous, of course. The worst thing he had on his record was a speeding ticket. But because he and Wade Stephenson had been talking so much lately, his past had been on his mind. He had never been punished for any of the things he had done or had passively been a part of, so when the FBI had showed up, he assumed the time had come to make wrong things right.

It was night now, and Robb was sipping from a tall glass of bourbon. He was watching fireflies begin to glow out in his yard, on and off, drifting across the darkness. He was thinking of Wade and all that they had discussed. It had been weird to have Wade Stephenson in his home—weirder still to find that he could not recall any reason why he had disliked Wade in high school. He'd simply laughed and mocked Wade because everyone else had. Even when the bullying had become physical and had, on one occasion, included a certain shampoo bottle, he had said nothing. He had not tried to stop it and he certainly hadn't turned any of his football playing friends in.

Instead, he'd simply lived his life with those memories, and the fact that he had never done a thing.

And he had lived with another memory, too. It was a memory he had almost told Wade about as they had exorcised their high school demons over burgers and beers on this very same back porch.

It was a memory concerning a girl named Claire Underhill. The memory was pasted to the walls of his brain and he thought of it at least three times a day. He did not recall the memory of what they had done to her with any sort of sexual fetishism or lust, though. He thought of it with regret so deep that it had carved a place into his heart—so deep that he had nearly reached out to Claire Underhill five years ago to beg for her forgiveness.

His mind was also orbiting around the three recent murders. He'd heard about two of them before the FBI agents had even shown up. And while they had said nothing of the sort when they had come from Wade, Rob couldn't help but wonder if they had arrested him because they thought *he* was the killer.

He supposed it made sense. A guy who had just come back into town—a guy who had been bullied by the recently murdered.

In all honesty, it made Robb wonder if Wade had been scoping him out. Had Wade been sizing him up, planning his next kill? Robb didn't think so. He hadn't shown any sort of anger toward him and, quite honestly, he just hadn't seemed like the type of dude that would be capable of murder.

Ah, but how do you know? a stubborn part of him spoke up. *Right now, you would say that there is no way in hell you are the type of man that is capable of rape. But look at what you did to that poor girl during your senior year of high school. Look at what you and those other four men did to Claire Underhill in that locker room …*

Robb downed the rest of the bourbon, knowing full well he would fill another tumbler with it. Hell, next time he might very well just bring the entire bottle out here.

In the back of his mind, he wondered if he should call the police to fill them in on his past. Luntz, Wells, and Nettles had all been there that night. And now they were dead. If Claire or someone associated with her was responsible for their deaths, surely he was on the list, too, right?

His hands trembled as he reached for the now-empty tumbler.

Behind him, from somewhere in the house, he heard his cell phone ringing. It was the fourth time it had rung in the last hour. He had ignored all of the calls, though. When the first one had come through, he had checked the number and, because he did not recognize it, let it go to voicemail.

He figured it was the cops or maybe even one of the agents who had shown up—maybe the agent who had kicked his fucking door down. They'd want to ask him more questions about Wade, and maybe about the three dead men he had once played high school football with. And he did not feel like talking about all of that. He figured if he talked about it enough and felt enough pressure and regret, he'd end up coming clean. And he was not ready for that… not yet. Hell, he might even take that filthy little secret to his grave.

The phone stopped ringing as he watched the fireflies continue to dance. He grabbed up the tumbler and headed back into the house. Only, the doorway was blocked.

There was a figure standing there shrouded in the darkness and shadow of the night and the slightly overhanging roof.

Confusion came before fear, and it cost him dearly.

"Who are—"

But then there was a swift movement, paralyzing pain in the side of his head, and a roaring blackness that swept him away.

CHAPTER THIRTY ONE

Doing sixty miles per hour in a thirty-five at night in a city she wasn't very familiar with was likely the most reckless thing Chloe had done in a while. Still, the surging adrenaline and sense that they were rushing against time was more powerful than the need for safety. While Rhodes remained silent, sitting upright and slightly antsy in her seat, Chloe could tell that her partner could sense the pressure of the moment, too.

Back at the academy, on the last day of her last year, one of her instructors had told them that there would be moments where everything in them would try to tell them something—would scream that they were about to step into something dangerous. The feeling surging through Chloe as she turned onto Robb's street was similar to that. She felt certain that whatever they were headed toward was going to mean the end of this case one way or another.

She pulled into the exact same spot she had parked in earlier in the day; the only difference this time was that Wade Stephenson's car was not there. They stepped out of the car quickly and sprinted to the front door. Chloe saw that Robb had installed a simple screen door to replace the one Rhodes had kicked in, presumably until he could make it to a hardware store or to hire someone to install a proper door tomorrow.

She tried opening the door and found it unlocked. They slipped in quietly, Chloe holding the door until it closed properly so it wouldn't bang shut as most screen doors tended to do. Perhaps it was just because the last time they visited the house was still fresh in her mind, but Chloe headed directly for the back patio. The rest of the house was dimly lit, the living room only illuminated by a single lamp that sat by the couch. The overhead oven lights were on, casting a warm sort of ambience to the kitchen. But Chloe barely noticed any of this.

What she did notice was that the back door leading to the patio was open. A woman's soft voice came whispering through it, her words muffled and hard to hear.

Chloe drew her weapon. Rhodes did the same as she came in beside her and also heard the voice.

Another two steps brought them to an unobstructed view of the open door. There was a woman standing over the fallen body of Thomas Robb. She had something in her right hand—it appeared to be a brick but it was hard to tell in the darkness. Whatever it was, she was clutching it tightly as she slowly dropped to her knees to crouch beside Robb's body.

"Freeze right there," Chloe said. "FBI. Drop the object in your hand."

The woman did freeze—but only for a second. She whipped around quickly, throwing the object in her hand. Chloe felt the wind of it whooshing by her head as she dodged to the right. Behind her, Rhodes let out a cry of pain and stumbled backward. In the second that followed, Chloe reoriented herself, prepared to take a shot at the woman, but there was suddenly a bulk of darkness in front of her as the woman threw herself at Chloe.

They went tumbling back into the side of the house. Chloe's back took the brunt of the force, slamming into the brick wall. As she rebounded, though, she was able to bring an elbow down on the woman's back. She was a small, frail woman but she took the hit like she was a broad-backed man. She flinched the slightest bit, though, opening a window of opportunity for Chloe. She drew up her right knee twice, one blow to the chest and the other to the face. She then drove her elbow into the woman's back again and this time when the elbow sunk into her lower back, she dropped like a sack of rocks.

The woman cried out as she went to the ground. Choe immediately fell on top of her, wrapped her arms around her neck and her legs around her waist. Rhodes came stumbling over hissing in pain as she took out her cuffs and applied them to the woman. Chloe released her hold and got back to her feet, her back aching.

"You okay?" she asked Rhodes.

"Don't know. That brick or whatever it was ... got me right in the shoulder ... it might be separated or something ..."

Chloe walked back over to the doorway, reached inside, and turned on the light on the back porch. The sudden light revealed all of the things that had gone unseen over the past thirty seconds or so.

First of all, Thomas Robb was still alive. His right leg was moving, as if trying to move into some sort of position to help him get to his feet. He had been hit on the right side of the head with the woman's weapon. He was bleeding from a large cut along his temple and his eye was swelling shut.

As for the weapon, it had indeed been a brick; it lay a few feet away from the woman on the porch floor.

The woman—presumably Claire Underhill—was writhing on the patio floor. She was crying and, it seemed, trying to say something. As Chloe hunkered down next to her, Rhodes partially fell into one of Robb's patio chairs. She was in tremendous pain and Chloe could tell just by looking at the state of her shoulder through her shirt that something was definitely not right.

Chloe took out her phone and called Anderson. Before he could even say "hello," Chloe interrupted him.

"Suspect in custody," she said. "We're at Thomas Robb's house. We're going to need medical attention for Mr. Robb and Agent Rhodes."

She ended the call, having made the entire call without Anderson speaking a single word.

"Are you Claire Underhill?" Chloe asked.

The woman stopped twitching and writhing for just a moment. She angled her head against the floor and looked at Chloe. There was pain—both physical and emotional—in her eyes. There was so much of it there that Chloe had to look away.

"Yes," the woman said.

Chloe looked the woman over, looking for any other weapons she might have on her. She thought back to the few wounds that had been found on Luntz, Wells, and Nettles. A brick could have been responsible for them all, but she wasn't sure.

As she tried to figure this out, she did find one single thing in Claire Underhill's pocket. It was in her back pocket, stuffed in almost randomly or so it seemed.

Chloe reached into the pocket and wasn't at all surprised when she pulled out a black athletic sock.

CHAPTER THIRTY TWO

Chloe was sitting in the hospital waiting room with Detective Anderson when the nurse came out of the second time. It was 10:15 at night and Chloe was starting to feel the weight of the day drag the energy out of her as she sat in the waiting room. But the nurse showing up put a spark of energy back into her. She was waiting on so many updates that it was dizzying. And Johnson was waiting for an update on Rhodes as well.

"Okay, so here's what we know so far," the nurse said, standing dutifully in front of them. "Mr. Robb has a fractured skull and is going to be here for at least a few days. He's mostly coherent and alert, so that's a good sign. Agent Rhodes dislocated her shoulder and there is quite a bit of swelling. She's being taken back for X-rays right now; her doctor thinks there's a chance she may need surgery, as it appears part of her shoulder may have fragmented."

"How serious is that?" Chloe asked.

"Not too bad. If it does require surgery, she should have full use of the shoulder back within a few weeks. But, again … we just don't know yet."

"What about Claire Underhill?" Anderson asked.

"Well, there's the single policeman still stationed outside of her door. She sustained minor injuries, including a broken nose. She's asked us twice to speak with one of the agents that arrested her. We needed to finish our evaluation first, of course."

"Is it okay to speak with her now?" Chloe asked.

"Yes. And I wish you'd do it now. She seems to be in a very bad emotional state."

"Thank you."

The nurse nodded and headed back the way she had come. Chloe took a deep breath and got to her feet. She started walking after the nurse, but Anderson stopped her.

"Want some company?" he asked.

"In all honesty, it would be nice. But we're talking about a woman that was taking vengeance on a gang rape from her teens. After all she's been through, I think the presence of an authoritative male is just going to make her less prone to talk."

"Good point. One more thing…"

"Yes?"

"DC to Baltimore….that's an hour and a half, right?"

"Maybe a little less. Why?"

"When this is all over and you head back, I think I'd like to take you out to dinner. You think that might be doable?"

She smiled at him. The force she had to put behind it reminded her just how tired she was. "That would be nice."

She left him with her sleepy smile and headed down the hallway to speak with the killer.

Claire Underhill had gauze under her nose and a dark bruise along the ridge of it. Even though Chloe had been the one to inflict those wounds, Underhill seemed to show no signs of resentment when Chloe entered the room. In fact, she gave a very hesitant smile—the sort a child might flash at a good-intentioned stranger.

"I was told you wanted to see me," Chloe said.

"How's the other agent?" Claire said without missing a beat.

"Her shoulder is banged up. She may need surgery, but she'll be okay."

Claire seemed to consider something for a moment, looking away from Chloe. "I know my life is over. The things I did … there's no coming back, right?"

"No. Likely not. I found the sock in your pocket and it connects it all."

"I don't intend to try getting out of it. I did it because they deserved it. They got away with this…this heinous crime. And no one batted an eye."

Chloe felt for her—she truly did. But the agent in her instantly got defensive at her justification of her actions.

"What did you need to see me for?" Chloe asked.

"I don't know, really. It's all falling on me now…the reality of what I've done. I'm not crazy and not out of my mind. I planned it. I did it. And I don't regret it."

There was a waver of emotion in her voice that Chloe thought might indicate otherwise, though.

"Why not just call the police?" Chloe asked.

"When? When it happened? Or when I decided I was going to take things into my own hands? My husband…he left me for another woman a few months ago. When that failed on him, he tried coming back to me. He tried sleeping with me when I started caving to him but I changed my mind. He decided he wanted it regardless of what I wanted…and I snapped. I stabbed him with a fingernail file and he left. And something about that…it triggered it all. It brought the past back up. I couldn't sleep…couldn't eat. I kept seeing those five boys…and I decided they'd lived as free men long enough. I decided that it was *their* turn to be scared and help-less—their turn to have that black athletic sock shoved into their mouth."

"Why the sock?" Chloe asked, her tone soft.

"The first guy—Richard Wells—he shoved a dirty sock in my mouth as a gag. By the time I spit it out the second time, they stopped caring. If I got loud, they'd just slam that locker door on me. By the time the third guy started, I had basically zoned out…unplugged…I wasn't even in my own body anymore, you know?"

Chloe felt her mouth going dry. Maybe she felt too much for this woman. And listening to her talk, she started to wonder what the repercussion of this all might be. She may get off without having to spend the rest of her life behind bars—especially if there was evidence of a cover-up from the school board and Claire's own family.

"Did Thomas Robb live?" Claire asked.

"Yeah. You fractured his skull, but he'll live."

Claire looked up to the ceiling and a tear trailed down out of the corner of her eye. Chloe wanted to say something to her but the idea of saying something touching or encouraging seemed wrong in light of what the woman had done.

So instead of saying anything, Chloe left the room. When she walked down the hallway back toward the waiting room, she realized that the conversation with Underhill had stirred her awake. With a cup of coffee, she might be able to make it through the night, staying awake to find out if Rhodes was going to need surgery or not.

When she returned to the waiting room, Anderson was still there. He was scrolling through his phone, looking up as she approached.

"How'd that go?" he asked.

"Strange." She eyed his phone and thought of her own, still dead in her pocket. She hadn't had a chance to charge it yet. "You mind if I use your phone to check my messages? I'm sure Johnson blew my phone up before he started calling yours to get to me."

"Knock yourself out," Anderson said, handing the phone to her.

It had been a while since Chloe had checked her voicemail from another phone, but the process came back to her easily enough. She got to her voicemail, fully expecting to have at least two or three messages from Johnson. She was rather surprised to find that she only had one. And it was not from Johnson.

It was from Danielle.

Her heart seemed to plummet through her body at the sound of her sister's voice. She felt her knees locking, her entire body going cold for a moment as she listened.

"Chloe... I've done something stupid and I don't know..."

By the time the message was over, tears were rolling down Chloe's face—which felt odd because of the absolute rage and disappointment that was cascading through her bloodstream.

She had been wrong all along. Her father had not kidnapped Danielle…

Danielle had kidnapped her father. And that, she realized with absolute clarity, was somehow worse.

"Agent Fine?"

It was Anderson, looking up at her with a baffled expression. He sat forward, as if unsure if he should stand or not. "Is everything okay?"

She wanted to listen to the message again, to make absolutely sure she had heard everything right. But she knew…she knew she'd heard it correctly. And she had no way of knowing how long ago the call had come until she charged her own phone to check the call history.

"Yeah," she said, wiping the tears away. She handed the phone back to Anderson, basically thrusting it at him. "I have to go…"

"Agent Fine…Chloe!"

The concern in his voice turned her heart a bit, but there was no way she could tell him what she had just heard—what her sister had gotten herself into. Danielle would be in jail by morning if she did.

"I'm okay," she said.

But she wasn't even out of his sight yet before she was running for the elevators.

CHAPTER THIRTY THREE

When Danielle managed to slip her hand out of one of the loops, she knew that it was just the beginning. She had no idea what her father was capable of. She knew she was going to have to kill him. She saw no other way out of it. Even if they both managed to make it out of Millseed alive, she was sure he would never leave them alone. He'd always be there, a part of their life that refused to go away no matter how much they wanted him to.

With her one hand freed, she started toying with the knot on her other arm. It was a bit tighter than the other but not by much. The knots had been poorly tied, probably because of the weakness in her father's arms from having had them stretched over his head for more than twenty-four hours.

But now he still stood in front of her, staring at her as if he had never seen her before. She saw glints of madness in his eyes—of a man who wasn't sure if he had anything to live for or not.

Still, she did not think he would kill her. He may hurt her—with more confessions or verbal abuse—but he would not kill her. Danielle thought of the hidden voice recorder, still hoping he had not found it.

"I'm going to leave here now," Aiden said. His arms were crossed and she thought he looked very tired, but also very determined. "I'll make an anonymous call to the police sometime soon, though I'm not sure when. I'll make sure it's soon."

"Why did you do it?" she asked. Yes, she wanted to know, but she also needed to keep him talking. She wasn't about to let him out of her sight.

"Many reasons," he said, answering her as if it didn't matter at all. "But you've already made up your mind, haven't you? I could give you every reason—could even have you thinking I might have a point—but you've already decided to hate me. You decided that a long time ago, didn't you?"

"Yes, and you made it so easy," she said, nearly hissing the comment.

She was no longer worried about what emotional state she showed him. She was angry and it made no sense to try convincing him otherwise. Besides… the anger made it much easier for her to concentrate on the knot that still held her left arm to the chair. She worked at the knot slowly, not wanting him to catch on to what she was doing. She could feel the rope slacking a bit, the folds of the knot coming undone little by little.

"Well, I certainly do wish you the best, Danielle," he said. "I truly wish you and I could have worked things out. There's so much of your mother in you… God, it pains me sometimes."

The final loop of the knot came undone. When the rope slid down and hit the floor, it made the tiniest little sound. But in the confines of the empty warehouse, it was like someone whispering from right beside them.

Aiden looked down. He saw the rope on the floor and a flicker of confusion touched his eyes and mouth. By the time he thought to act on what he was seeing by rushing forward to tie her to the chair again, Danielle was already in motion.

In an awkward half-sitting-half-standing position, Danielle brought the chair around in a wide arc. Aiden saw it a split second too late. He was bringing his arm up to block the blow just as it reached its mid-swing point. The chair slammed into his side up high at an angle. One of the legs caught him in the jaw, the other hitting his shoulder. The old chair broke into several pieces upon contact, but the blow had done enough. It sent him stumbling to the left, instantly reaching for his jaw.

Danielle wanted to follow up, to find one of the stray pieces of the shattered chair to beat him with. But she then saw her bag sitting at her feet, saw the pile of pallets a few yards away. She managed to allow logic to win the fight over her need for vengeance, picking the bag up and grabbing the recorder from under the pallet and running for the door. If she could make it to her car, she'd go to the police. Sure, that would give her father an opportune chance to make a run for it, but where the hell was he going to go? Millseed was in the middle of nowhere. A manhunt would turn him up within a very short amount of time.

She dashed through the doorway, putting the recorder in her bag before zipping it up and slipping it over her shoulder. She was trying to do too much at once, though; as she came out of the building, her right foot slipped on the loose dirt in front of the slaughterhouse. She went to the ground hard, the breath knocked out of her. She got to her knees at once, wincing through the pain as she managed to get to her feet.

By the time she started running again, her father was right behind her—almost within arm's reach. Danielle sprinted off into the night, headed toward her car. The field that separated the slaughterhouse from her car looked like an endless black ocean under a cloudy night sky. As she looked across it, she then realized that her father had no idea where she had parked her car. If she led him right to it and he managed to overpower her, that could be very bad news. The last thing she needed was to be stranded out here with her father driving off in her car.

Instead of heading directly for the car, she angled off to the right. She cut through the field, headed toward the forest. She figured if she could get far enough ahead of him, she could hide for a while, wait for him to get a good distance away, and *then* she'd head for her car.

"Danielle, there's no need to run," he bellowed from behind her. "We can work this out! What are you doing?"

She didn't let his words slow her down. She ran through the field, finally coming to the edge of the woods. When she stepped into them, it was like a totally different world of darkness. The scant light from the clouded quarter moon was mostly blocked by the branches and leaves. Still, her eyes had managed to adjust to the lightlessness of the night. It took only a few moments for them to get adjusted to the forest. Still, as she forged ahead, the shapes of trees seemed to come out of nowhere. Low-hanging branches scratched her face and her shoulders struck the edges of trees on a few occasions.

"Damn it, Danielle, please stop!"

Keep talking, asshole, she thought. Every word he spoke let her know exactly where he was. And as far as she could tell, she had gotten a good distance away from him. If she could find some huge tree to hide behind for a few moments, she'd then make a quiet dash for her car. She just needed to—

There was sudden resistance at her right foot, followed by a wrenching pain. She was sprinting when it happened, causing her to fall forward. She struck the ground hard, dimly aware that her stupid foot had snagged itself in a root or something. And if the pain was any indication, she had broken her foot, sprained her ankle, or something. The pain was sudden and intense, but she was also quite sure the adrenaline of the situation was muting it a bit.

She cried out, trying to bite it back but not able to. She had no doubt that it had been loud enough to alert her father. She tried getting to her feet but her right foot refused to take on any weight. She felt herself falling again, reaching out to a nearby tree to stay up.

As she leaned against it, she could hear her father's footfalls. He had indeed heard her cry of pain and was closing in on her. Danielle tried hobbling forward only to fall again. This time, she let out a curse, knowing that her father had already found her anyway.

By the time she had rolled over onto her back, trying to slide into a hiding position by the tree she had been leaning against, she saw his shape. He was mostly hidden in the dark, though a sliver of chalky moonlight fell through the branches to paint his face. In that moment, Aiden Fine looked almost like a ghost.

"What did you hurt?" he asked her.

"Go to hell."

"Danielle, this is stupid."

"You admitted to it. You told me … you killed her."

"I did. But that's in the past. We can move past this. I think we *have* to …"

With that, he did something she would have never expected. He knelt down to her, kissed her on the cheek, and then placed his right knee hard into her chest. "And now that I have you here, unable to go anywhere, we're going to talk it out. You have to see it my way, Danielle."

Danielle realized two things in that moment. First, he would never leave her alone until she either forgave him or managed to look past what he had done. Second, she was now certain that something had come unhinged in her father. She didn't know when it had happened specifically, but she could hear lunacy in his voice.

The fact that he kept increasing the pressure on her chest did not help. He was all but pushing down his whole weight into that one knee, pushing the air out of her and making every muscle in her chest groan.

"Will you listen now, Danielle?"

She thought of the gun she had brought. She had no idea if it was still in the slaughterhouse or in her pack. Regardless, it was out of her reach either way, as the pack was now crushed between her back and the forest floor.

She slapped at the forest floor with her hands. She hoped to find a root or outcropping of rock, something to help pull her away from him. He was old and a little frail, sure, but he still outweighed her by about thirty pounds and Danielle had never been very physically strong.

"She never understood me," Aiden said. "She never cared to understand me. It was just you girls … you and Chloe, that's all she cared about."

Danielle dug her hands into dirt and foliage, trying to pull away. But there was no budging, no way to escape. She clawed and clawed at the dirt, clawed for any hope of …

Her left hand fell on something hard, oddly textured, and cool to the touch. She covered it with her hand and found that she could just barely palm it. It was a rock, a loose rock that was buried in the soil.

As the pressure against her chest increased, Danielle screamed. Not for help necessarily, but out of frustration. And when she freed the softball-sized rock from the ground, it was a scream of anger and triumph.

She brought her arm up in a stabbing-like motion, straight up toward his face. Had she been using only her closed fist, it might have struck his jaw and forced his teeth to clink together.

But, because there was a large rock in her clutches, it did much more. She felt his jaw shift wide to the left. She not only felt but *heard* something snap and then crunch.

The weight was removed from her chest for a moment. It then came again, but briefer... softer. He was falling forward onto her, dazed and limp. Danielle acted on impulse, swinging the rock around again, this time in a full-on punch. It connected with the side of her father's head. There was a meaty *thud* as his body tilted hard to the right and fell to the ground.

Danielle scurried away as fast as she could, crying now. Her hand hurt like hell, though not as badly as her right foot. The rock had done a number of her father for sure, but it had also damaged her hand.

She lay there, looking over at her father's motionless body. He was moaning in a low throaty sound, but he was not moving. Danielle slowly sat up. She looked at the rock in her hand, smeared with some of her father's blood.

She let out a little moan of her own and felt herself trembling.

She listened to him moaning. It was pain. It was an attempt to speak.

Danielle hefted the rock in her hand as she managed to get to her knees. She slid over toward her father and when she raised the rock for a final blow, she imagined the waning moonlight reflected from it.

She focused on that, trying to find the poetry of it as she summoned up the nerve to take the final, killing blow.

CHAPTER THIRTY FOUR

Chloe sped back to the Central District precinct and gathered up the few files and personal items she had left there. She then hurried back out to the car where she had plugged her phone in to charge when she had left the hospital. As she ran through the precinct, she noticed quite a few lingering stares, but she did not let them bother her. In fact, she barely noticed them at all. She was in a different world, going about her own task and seeing other people as nothing more than blurs and vague shapes.

Back in the car, she drove recklessly as she also used her phone to do several things. She'd already tried calling Danielle's phone several times, to the same results she'd gotten before venturing into Baltimore. First, she checked her call history and saw that the message from Danielle had come five and a half hours ago. So if she was going to do something stupid, chances were she would have done it by now. She was crying again but didn't even realize it. Wiping tears away and honking her way through a stoplight, she then Googled the town of Millseed, Texas—a place she had never heard of before.

As it turned out, it was a small town about eighty-five miles outside of Dallas. After finding this out, she pulled up her Expedia app and scrolled through to find the soonest flight out of Baltimore into Dallas or anywhere remotely close to it. In this regard, luck was on her side. There was a red-eye flight out flying into Dallas in three hours with no connecting flights. She booked the flight, making a list of things she knew she was going to have to answer for within the next twenty-four hours or so.

With the flight booked, Chloe called back the number Danielle had called her from out of Millseed. It rang ten times and then clicked to a dead thrum of a line. *Probably a public phone at a convenience store or something that's closed at this hour,* she thought.

With that done, she dropped her phone for a moment as the exit for the airport looked into view on her right. She was still speeding even though she knew the flight wasn't for another three hours.

She called almost six hours ago, she thought. *Add three more to that while I wait for the flight, another three or so for the flight itself, and then driving time from Dallas to Millseed. Jesus... is it even worth rushing?*

"Yes it is," she said to the empty car.

She picked her phone back up and placed another call, this one to Rhodes's phone. She was expecting to leave a voicemail message but was surprised when Rhodes actually answered.

"Fine... good to hear from you."

"How are you doing?" Chloe asked, already feeling guilty for leaving Rhodes behind while she was in pain. Hearing her partner's voice was an awful reminder that she would be there alone, in a hospital with no one there by her side. Sure, Anderson would be there but he already had his hands full with processing Claire Underhill whenever she got out of the hospital.

"I'm good," Rhodes said. "Just about to head into X-rays. The nurse in the room right now seems pissed that I'm taking a call. I think they'd be okay if you came back."

"I can't. Rhodes... my sister called. And between you and me, I think she might be in some pretty big danger. I have to go."

Rhodes was quiet for a while before she finally responded. "I get it. And I think you need to go. But... what am I supposed to tell Johnson?"

"I'll handle that," she said. "But it might be a while. If he does reach out to you, just tell him some version of the truth—that I had a family emergency I had to take care of."

"He knows the deal with you and your sister," Rhodes pointed out. "Chloe... you could get into serious trouble over this."

"I know. But it's my sister. I have to."

"I know. Just be careful."

After ending the call, Chloe tossed the phone into the passenger seat. She gripped the steering wheel and stared ahead into the night. With all of the items on her to-do list knocked out, she was able to focus on the only thing that mattered to her in that moment: getting to ger sister and hoping she wasn't too late to save her from either a terrible mistake or, God forbid, something much worse.

Sitting in the airport and waiting for her flight time to roll around was excruciating. She could feel each second wasted, one more second for Danielle and her father to come to whatever epilogue they saw fit. It was, Chloe realized, a no-win situation. Either one of them would come out of this dead or there would be some sort of forced and marginalized reconciliation.

Chloe pounded down two coffees while she waited. She was well aware that the last bit of sleep she had gotten had been on a holding cell cot; it had been about five hours of sleep, and not a very restful one. She also knew she would not be able to sleep on the plane, though she wished she could. The anxiety of knowing there was nothing she could do except wait and rely on a plane and a rent-a-car once she got to Dallas made her feel impossibly helpless.

Twenty minutes before the scheduled boarding call at 2:45 in the morning, she got a text. She checked it, daring to hope it would be Danielle. She was not surprised when it was not her sister, though. Instead, it was Rhodes.

No surgery required, the text read. They are releasing me in the morning, in this messed up sling. Not that I could go anywhere anyway. I assume you took the car?

Chloe knew she should feel guilty about this, too, but she simply didn't have the capacity to feel it. She replied: **Sorry. It's parked in Lot B, Space 27 at the airport.**

With that, she pocketed her phone again. She would have just turned it off if it weren't for the slight hope that Danielle might try to get in touch with her again. She wondered how early Johnson would get into the office in the morning, and how long it would take for him to find out what she was up to.

It was a scary thought, and Rhodes had been right. What she was doing now could very well cost her job.

But apparently, she was too tired to care much about that, either. Because when they called her flight to start boarding, her job was the last thing on her mind. All she could think about was her sister and the many things that could have already gone wrong.

Chapter Thirty Five

Dawn lit up the Dallas/Fort Worth area as the plane landed. As she had expected, Chloe had been unable to sleep during the flight, though she had managed to zone out, staring into the early morning darkness as the plane headed south and finding a state almost like sleep. But the moment the wheels screeched against the runway upon landing, Chloe found that she was wide awake.

The next half an hour was almost as excruciating as wasting those three hours in the airport in Baltimore. Dealing with a rental car agency first thing in the morning was on her list of the most miserable experiences on the planet. And because she was wary about using her FBI credentials, everything had to be done with her own money, and her own ID. She nearly laughed in a maniacal way when she imagined Johnson looking over an expense report and finding that she had paid for this little adventure on the bureau's dime.

She'd *certainly* lose her job then.

She kept this in mind as she headed northeast toward the town of Millseed, which, according to Google maps, was exactly ninety-one miles away from the airport. She only allowed herself to speed seven miles over the speed limit—but up to fifteen over when she was on the interstate, which was not a lot as she headed deep into the more rural area of the eastern part of the state.

As she closed in on Millseed, the bright morning sun seemed to promise pleasant things, but the broiling in her guts told her otherwise.

Her cell phone rang at 7:21. She fumbled for it, veering across the lane and thankful there was no oncoming traffic. Now, less than

187

fifteen miles from Millseed, she was on a mostly dead two-lane that seemed to shoot straight into a distant line of trees.

The call was not from Danielle, as she had hoped. Instead, Director Johnson's name was on the display. She nearly answered it, figuring it might be better to go ahead and get it over with. But no... she had to be one hundred percent focused on what she was about to find in Millseed. Maybe a dead sister. Maybe a dead father. Maybe something even worse—something she hadn't even thought to imagine just yet.

Instead of answering the phone, she shut it down and dropped it back into the passenger seat.

She continued down the two-lane until she came to a four-way intersection. Her directions told her to head straight, which she did without coming to a complete stop. Passing by the intersection was somehow fitting. She felt herself leaving behind any choice to walk away. She was in it deep now, less than ten minutes away from entering the town her sister had called her from, confessing that she had gotten into water too deep to get out of.

She entered into Millseed at 7:28. She knew this by the small sign, partially hidden by a tree branch along the side of the road that read, simply: Millseed. There was no town nor even a single building to greet her. There were just trees, the two-lane, and the morning sun. Another mile down the road, which she blasted beyond doing ninety at this point, she saw a convenience store coming up on her left. Just before that, though, she saw another road sign. This one indicated that State Road 14 was coming up on the right—the road Danielle had mentioned in her short but emotional message.

Chloe slowed considerably as she passed the convenience store. As she did so, she spotted the pay phone sitting neglected in the far corner. She wondered if that very phone had rung ten times and then stopped when she had called the number Danielle had called her from. She pictured Danielle standing there, clutching the receiver as she wept, and her heart broke.

When she came up on State Road 14 less than half a mile further down the road, she turned so quickly and so fast that she felt the back of the car fishtail out into the other lane a bit. She replayed Danielle's message in her head: *a big empty concrete building on State Road 14.*

With that lodged in her head, Claire Underhill and her three victims (as well as the fourth she had nearly claimed) were distant memories. It all could have happened in some other world, to some other woman.

This was even more the case when, about five miles further down the road, she saw a large concrete building sitting off on the side of the road. There was what looked to have once been a parking lot in front of it, but it had gone to ruin. Now it was nothing more than speckled patches of cracked pavement, tall weeds, and dirt. The building itself sat about fifty yards off of the road, bordered by a thick grove of forest.

Chloe saw no sign of a car or that anyone was there, but she knew that meant nothing. She turned into the sorry excuse for a road that led to the building. Like the deteriorated parking lot, the road was really nothing more than a memory. But thanks to the glorious morning light, she could clearly see freshly worn spots along the edge, where something heavy had pressed the overgrowth down the slightest bit.

Someone had been here recently.

She made her way to the building and saw an old sign that had been knocked over. It read Warner and Mitchum Slaughterhouse. The paint, ironically, had once been red but had faded into a pale and chipping pink. Here, the would-be parking lot was essentially nothing. There was only dirt and scraggly grass, growing all the way to the building.

She pulled farther up, parking her car behind the building. She had hoped to find a car there—hoping for Danielle's car—but she saw no such thing. It was just her…and she was starting to think she had either made a mistake and was at the wrong place or that Danielle *had* been here, but she was too late.

Still, she was here. She might was well get out and look around. If nothing else, it could potentially give her some answers.

From the back of the building, there were two possible entrances: a loading door that sat above a tall, crumbling platform, or a smaller door at the very edge of the building that had likely once been an employee entrance. She chose the smaller door, not at all surprised to find it unlocked yet nearly rusted shut in the frame.

When she opened the door, she stepped inside right away. From the first footfall, she could tell the place was empty. But there was also the sense of stirring in the air, the feel of a previously forgotten place having recently been disturbed. It was in the smell of the dust, something fresh among all of the neglect.

The back door had led her to a small room that she guessed had once been a break room of sorts. There was a small table with a few old chairs around it. But there was nothing else. She left this room and came to a much larger room. There were chains hanging from the walls and ceiling, old rusted vines that hung down loosely. There were also a few ropes hanging among the chains.

One of the ropes hung down lower than the others. Underneath it, she saw an absolute mess of footprints. She hunkered down next to them but could not tell anything about the size of them. All she knew for certain was that they were very fresh.

She got to her feet and looked over the rest of the room. There was a large stack of old pallets in the corner. Several trails of footprints led around this stack, too. Some went back and forth to the chain.

Oh my God… something terrible had to have happened…

She ran out of the room and into the next, an even larger room with drains in the floor. Chains and hooks hung from the ceiling, but they had long been retired, not hanging down like the ones in the previous room. She had no time to study it, though. The room was empty. If Danielle and her father had been here, they were gone.

"Shit."

She had no idea where to go from here, but she had to move. She had to do something. She raced back through the building, through each of the rooms and back outside. She ran to her car, opened the door, and nearly got in.

That's when she saw the fresh indentations in the tall grass behind the building. They seemed to have come from around the front of the building, cutting to the back and then through the field at an angle. It was hard to tell how fresh the trail through the tall weeds was, or if it had been made by a human at all. It could have been a deer for all she knew.

Maybe, but you know better, some wider and more urgent part of her spoke up.

She sprinted from her car to the little path that had been trampled down through the field. She could instantly tell the trail led into the woods. She could imagine Danielle running into those woods, bringing that God-awful nightmare to mind. Chloe could see it all over again, could hear the—

"Help."

Chloe froze. She turned her head to the left, listening. Had she really heard that? A woman's voice, crying for help in a soft, desperate voice. Or had she imagined it?

"Is someone there?" Chloe asked. She did not scream it, but raised her voice considerably.

The reply was almost immediate. "Yes. Please. Help."

It was Danielle's voice. She was certain of it.

No longer concerned about remaining quiet or stealthy, Chloe ran directly into the forest. She did not follow the slightly beaten path, but tore through the taller grass. "Danielle, where are you?"

"Here…"

It was weak and dry. A thousand different images passed through Chloe's mind. She pictured Danielle with multiple bullet wounds, barely hanging on for life, soaked in blood and weak. Panic soared in Chloe as she made her way to the edge of the forest and crossed over from the sunlit field into the morning shadows of the forest.

"Keep talking, Danielle," she said, trying to keep her voice calm.

"I'm here… I'm hurt but okay."

The voice came from the right and slightly deeper into the forest. Chloe ran that way, hearing Danielle continue to speak.

"I'm so sorry, Chloe. I thought I could do it. I thought I knew what I was doing…"

And then she started to cry. It was an uncontrollable bout of weeping that came through the forests like a wailing wind. It made it very easy for Chloe to follow, tearing past trees and jumping over stumps and fallen limbs.

And then she finally came to Danielle. She was propped up against a large oak tree, her right foot propped up on a fallen log. She looked filthy and weak, but still within her senses. The look of absolute love and relief that came over her face when Chloe saw her filled Chloe with a love that almost washed away the panic that came when she saw her father.

His body was lying about five feet away from Chloe. His face was turned away from them, and he did not appear to be moving.

Chloe knelt by her sister and was unable to stop from kissing her on the forehead. "Are you okay? Did he hurt you?"

"He didn't. He tried, I think. But it's my foot. Pretty sure it's broken. I couldn't get away and just stayed here, praying you'd show up. I just…"

She started sobbing again and Chloe pulled her close. As they hugged, she looked over to her father. It was hard to tell, but she thought she could see the very slight rise and fall of his back as he took in shallow breaths. But maybe not…

She moved over to him, unsure of what she hoped to find. She found his eyes closed and two large abrasions on his head. She checked his vitals and was surprised when a lump of sadness rose up in her throat.

She turned back to Danielle, trembling slightly, and asked: "How long has he been dead?"

Chapter Thirty Six

Chloe looked Danielle's foot over and was fairly certain it was not broken—not in any visible way. It could be fractured, but she still thought it was only a very bad sprain. It had swollen terribly and the bruise had gone a dark purple shade.

"You're sure he's head?" Danielle asked. "I hurt him enough to get him off of me, but when I tried giving one more blow with that rock, I...I couldn't do it."

"Yeah, he's gone," Chloe said. She had seen the specifics but did not share them with her sister. One of the two blows she had delivered with the rock had not only broken his nose, but obliterated it. The force had shattered his skull, too.

"How much trouble am I going to be in?" Danielle asked.

"I don't know," Chloe said. She was already thinking of ways to explain this away, trying to come up with fanciful explanations. With her father dead it would, of course, be easier to come up with a story that would not be contested.

"My car," Danielle said, almost randomly. "Parked in the back. There's water in it. Can you grab it?"

Chloe wasted no time, doing it right away. While she was there, she also looked around in the glove box for a painkiller for Danielle's foot. There was nothing of the sort, though she did find a partially eaten bag of Chex Mix. She grabbed the water and the snack and ran back to Danielle.

"We can get out of this, I think," Chloe said. "We'll have to lie. But...it might be hard."

"But I got him," Danielle said. She reached into the backpack that had been sitting against the tree beside her. Slowly, she drew out the voice recorder and handed it to Chloe. "I was afraid he would have found where I hid it and turned it off, but he didn't. But it's on there, Chloe. His admission…"

Chloe nodded, feeling fury and some weird sort of relief in equal measure.

"Are you mad at me?" Danielle asked.

It seemed like a ridiculous question—the sort of thing a kid might ask an adult after they've broken a vase. The truth of the matter was that Chloe was not mad at Danielle. She was very disappointed, but not angry. But that was not a discussion she wanted to have right now. She ignored the question as she cycled through the multiple ways she could get her sister out of this mess.

"I need you to think hard," Chloe said. "Did you talk to anyone in town? Maybe when you called me?"

"No. I made a point not to."

"When was the last time you got gas for your car?"

"I don't remember. But it was later at night, somewhere just before we got into Texas, I think."

Chloe nodded, looking around the forest. She knew that there would be a trail linking her to a visit to Texas. There was no way anyone would know *where* in Texas, but she could be tracked to the airport rental car desk. She was going to have to play it very cautiously if she wanted both of them out of this unscathed.

"Okay, so we're going to be here for a while," Chloe said. "Do you have a change of clothes?"

"Yeah. One. In the back seat of my car."

"I'm going to change into them and take your car into town. I'm going to get some ice and ibuprofen for your foot. I'll also grab some food and water. If I can get lucky enough to find a shovel, I'm going to buy it."

"What for?"

"We have to bury his body."

The weight of it coming out of her mouth was immense. *This is what this situation has become,* she thought. *There's no coming back from this…*

194

"But if there's a manhunt or something, won't dogs find it?" Danielle asked.

"Probably. So we're going to have to mask it. I need to find something dead. The bigger the better."

"Chloe, that's—"

But Chloe shut her out. She had a plan in mind and there was no going back. She had her gun in the car, and she supposed she could find something in these woods. A deer would be perfect. Hell, in a backwoods town like this, there were probably dead animals all over the sides of the back roads. Maybe she'd get lucky.

"Chloe."

"What?" she asked, almost snapping at Danielle.

"Thank you. I know I shouldn't have done this, and I know you put a lot at risk to come here looking for me."

She was right, but Chloe wasn't ready to go through all of that with her just yet. She sat down by her sister, working out the last few details of her plan.

"It's okay," Chloe said, taking her sister's hand in her own. "It's going to be okay."

For a moment, she saw the two of them as those two little girls, sitting on the front stoop while policemen walked in and out of their apartment on the day their mother had been killed.

"How do you know that?" Danielle asked.

"Because we've finally escaped him," Chloe said, nodding over to the lifeless shape of their father. "He's out of our lives now and everything is going to be okay."

When the words came out of her mouth, Chloe believed it.

And that was perhaps the most concerning thing of all.

Now Available for Pre-Order!

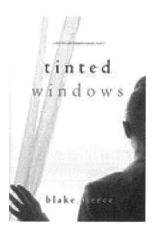

TINTED WINDOWS
(A Chloe Fine Psychological Suspense Mystery—Book 6)

"A masterpiece of thriller and mystery. Blake Pierce did a magnificent job developing characters with a psychological side so well described that we feel inside their minds, follow their fears and cheer for their success. Full of twists, this book will keep you awake until the turn of the last page."
—Books and Movie Reviews, Roberto Mattos (re Once Gone)

TINTED WINDOWS (A Chloe Fine Mystery) is book #6 in a new psychological suspense series by bestselling author Blake Pierce, whose #1 bestseller Once Gone (Book #1) (a free download) has over 1,000 five-star reviews.

When a popular personal trainer is murdered in a high-end sub-urb, FBI VICAP Special Agent Chloe Fine, 27, is summoned to sift through a small town filled with cheating spouses and figure out who may have wanted him dead—and why.

Behind the manicured lawns, Chloe learns, lie broken marriages, lonely spouses, secrets, and endless lies—all hiding behind the veil of perfection. Beneath the carefully built façade of a polished, upstanding community lies a populace dishonest to its core.

What secrets led to this man's being murdered?

And who will be next to die?

An emotionally wrought psychological suspense with layered characters, small-town ambiance and heart-pounding suspense, TINTED WINDOWS is book #6 in a riveting new series that will leave you turning pages late into the night.

Book #7 in the Chloe Fine series will also be available soon.

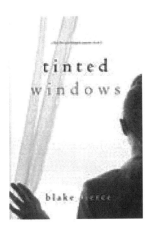

TINTED WINDOWS
(A Chloe Fine Psychological Suspense Mystery—Book 6)

Did you know that I've written multiple novels in the mystery genre? If you haven't read all my series, click the image below to download a series starter!